MW01172997

Acknowledgments

I most definitely have to thank a few people for this book, I guess that's what you do when you know that without them you know it never would have happened.

To my parents, Lori and Hank Pelt, for always letting me be myself no matter how much of a quirky, annoying, cheeseball middle child with a twisted sense of humor I was and still am...you have helped me through a lot in life and I will be eternally grateful.

My sisters Laura and KyKy...thank you for always accepting my dreams and passions...no matter how much we disagree (because that's what siblings do) know that I love you to pieces!

To Sheila Maria - not Marie - Cannon, thank you sooooo much for the cover art on this book. I had the image in my head and you brought it out. It turned out exactly the way I wanted. I thank you.

Last but not least, a MAJOR thank you to Myke...the love of my life, my Babe, my Puddin' for encouraging me to even start this journey and to keep motivating me to continue with it even when I felt there was no way I could achieve it. Without your love and support through this whole thing, it would have been just another failure to add to the books. Thank you from the bottom of my heart.

Prologue

'Step Right Up.'

The headline that started my journey that landed me where I am today.

A journey that I have not shared with any other soul on this Earth, not the full story that is.
I sit here in this damp and cold dungeon of a room lit only by candlelight as I have done many times before, attempting to get my story onto paper but never able to find the words. While often wondering if she's still out there, living her life.

A happy, fulfilled life.

Free of me.

I have always wanted to get the thoughts out. Those that have tortured my head for so long, an explanation as to why I am the way I am, how I became this monster. Most importantly, why I have done the things I have done.

Yet as I dip my quill into the black ink and begin to spill my soul, I can't help but wonder if anyone would care. Why would anyone take the time to read the going ons of a madman?

Of the monster they so feared and were so delighted to have presumed dead.

That's what they all branded me.

A monster.

Every last one of them. Except her. For years I have been trapped in this fog, the walls themselves seem to come alive right before my eyes. I don't know if I will ever be able to find my way out but I hope you will read my side and let me set the story straight.

My name is Oscar Melvin, but I am more commonly known to the world as Jack the Ripper.

Chapter One

My name is Oscar Melvin. I know that much about myself. I was not always the cruel and vile man you have heard about, I was molded, shaped, and beaten into it.

I was born into a very high society and very wealthy family, at least from what I can remember, it's been years since I have seen any of them. Let me not get ahead of myself. I was born in the year eighteen-sixty to Martin and Anna Melvin, two of the most famous and prominent entertainers of the time. They were a wonderful duo in which Mother sang and danced while Father performed magic and all kinds of wonderful mystical acts that would blow the roof right off of this place. They packed theatres and received standing ovations every night. I remember sneaking out of my room to watch them rehearse their next act until all hours of the night.

From the moment my parents laid eyes on me, they despised me.

You see, I was born with a rare disfigurement to my head that made my mother shudder at the very sight of me. I was always treated differently, kept home for my schooling, hidden away in the small den I had for a room. I wasn't even treated as one of the family, but more as one of the house workers. It also led them to deem me a monster. Living in a family of show folk, vanity plays a large role in the personal and professional affairs. Having a child with a physical abnormality made them fear it would have a negative impact on their social standing and therefore ruin the family name thus tearing it down from it's high standing.

My childhood was not a very pleasant one.

One of my first vivid memories is from when I was four, this time my parents were having a rather large ball, an important one to find investors to fund their next show. I was forced upstairs and shoved into my brother, Peter's room with only a few small scraps from dinner. They didn't want their guests to see me. I could hear the music from the live band my mother had called in to entertain floating up. Lively conversation and laughter filled the house as it often did when my parents threw these gatherings. It always sounded so marvelous. Some time in the evening, I became horribly thirsty. I held off for as long as I could, but when I felt as if my throat was about to burst, I decided against my better judgment to go downstairs for a glass of water.

As quietly as I could, I pulled the heavy wooden door to my brother's room open, taking a quick glance into the dark hallway to be sure it was clear of any wandering party guests. I quickly slid out of the room, hugging the wall tightly as I could and keeping an eye over the banister. Down the stairs I crept and just as I thought I had successfully achieved my slow and steady race to the kitchen, a woman bounded around the corner and bumped into me.

"Oh, Sor-," It took just one look at my face to begin her screaming. The music came to a stop and the entire room of people turned to face us. I was immediately grabbed by one of our footmen who rushed me through the kitchen and out into the alleyway behind our house. My father was fuming. I was left out there until the end of the party, dreading the moment that it was over, hoping it would last all night.

Once the last party guest took their leave, my father came out to the yard where I had been pondering what my punishment would be. I tried to explain my reasoning but Father was not interested in what I had to say, I still received a handful of lashes from his belt. He locked me outside for the rest of the night so I could think about why I had disobeyed, how I could have jeopardized everything my parents had worked so hard for. I ended up sleeping with the dogs to keep warm. Even now, I sit here, I can still recall the look upon my father's face. A look of disgust that I had gone against his order to stay hidden from sight. He told me that he and my mother had to tell everyone that I must have been a stray who snuck in the back door to spy on the good time everyone was having.

As a child, my siblings, two brothers named Peter and James, and a sister named Elizabeth were not allowed to play with me. My brothers would bully me, however, and call me names. They beat me up a lot and some days they would act like I did not even exist. I preferred the days where they ignored me, at least I could have peace and quiet. Left to just sit by myself, not being ridiculed. On those days I was safe from the beatings and being called a freak, I let myself feel as close to normal as I could on those days. There was one morning when I woke up extra early to help get breakfast prepared and the house tidied for Mother and Father to accept business calls from potential funders for their next show, my brother James was waiting for me. I'm not sure what I did to upset him but he was not happy with me. He tackled me to the ground and began slapping me in the face. I fought back just enough to get free, taking off outside, only to have my head dunked into the cold water in the trough we kept outside for the dogs to drink from. James only stopped when one of the housemaids came out from the house and pulled him off of me. I was grateful for the servants in my home. They always welcomed and accepted me, I was grateful for them as they stuck up for me and protected me in such a way that my own family did not. It was the only time I ever felt welcome.

Other than the large deformity on my head, I was a healthy and normal child. I was considered beyond average in my schooling and I always received excellent

4

marks with my tutors. It was the only time that my father would show any sense of pride towards me, causing me to work as hard as I could on my school work which only made my brothers pick at me even more. They preferred to act up and play through their study time while I took it upon myself to get educated as best as I could because as much as I wanted to take over the family business. Even at five, I knew I wanted to entertain as I had seen it bring my parents so much joy. I also knew I would never be able to use the family name nor would I have the looks to fall back on like my brothers, but being more intelligent did not sit well with them. Being better than something was never to their liking.

In my free time I played outside, mostly by myself or I would read. Our book selection was grand, although, we did not have many books for children my age around, so I mostly read books on business, education, and other subjects to help further my learning. I did anything to please my parents, learning to play the piano for my mother as it was her favorite instrument. She loved music and was always going to the opera and concerts. I worked day and night to perfect my talents just to see her smile at me. After a couple of years, I even learned how to compose my own music.

I learned a lot of trades as I was left to my own devices. One being cooking and I was glad I had the opportunity to have learned it because most days, I had to prepare the meals for the family. Even though I was not able to sit at the table and eat with them, I was always given a small plate that I could take to the kitchen with the servants.

I remember some of the best evenings were when Elizabeth would sneak into the small den that was turned into a room for me. We would make forts out of sheets and tell stories of far off places, where we wanted to travel to in the future, asking me to tell her about the places I would read about in my books. Elizabeth would speak of the romance she always dreamed of, one of the few subjects I knew very little about. She would always save some of her dinner to share with me as I would often be hungry as a result of not getting enough to eat at dinner. Some nights I was required to help serve the family, not an easy feat for a child of six. If I did anything incorrectly or not to their liking, my hands were swatted with a spoon. Elizabeth became my saving grace. She was always so kind to me, even if she knew she would get scolded for it. She would often tell me how when she was old enough, she planned to leave home and never look back. You would never have able to tell she was so unhappy until those nights when it was just the two of us. She had such an upbeat glow about her and smiled everywhere she went. Just thinking about her now brings a smile to my face.

As I got older and was more able to do things on my own, my mother and father began making me wear what I suppose you would call hats and masks over my face when we would go out in public. They were usually just old vegetable burlap sacks that made my face itch terribly and often caused me to break out into horrible rashes that would leave red blotches all over my face. I almost did not mind because I was just happy to be out with the family. Once again, Elizabeth came to my rescue. She learned a lot on how to make costumes and from our

5

mother to help with clothes for my parents' shows. She had a talent for sewing. She came to my room one evening with a round hatbox, black with the letters OM on top in red. When I opened it, there was a beautifully made black top hat with a red ribbon around the base that Lizzie had made for me all on her own. I absolutely loved it, it fit me perfectly and was of the best quality. I wore it everywhere I went after that, even though when I wore it out into public, I would get odd looks from people. Who could blame them? The hat was pretty extravagant for a child of seven. I loved my hat but I despised that I was forced to wear it. I soon realized who the real monsters were and I was not one of them.

One day that will always stick with me, I was around ten years old at the time the very first time my mother sent me out completely on my own. My father became very ill with an aggressive fever and ended up bedridden. My mother, not knowing what he had come down with was afraid to leave his side, much less the house, sitting by the bedside with him as much as she could to care for him. I was sent out for his medicine and items to help my father stay comfortable in his time of illness. Among those items was the daily post.

That was the day that my life changed forever.

My stomach still flips as I think of the excitement that coursed through my veins.

I gripped the post in my hands clenching it tightly between my fingers. Staring in amazement at the words that were printed across the top.

Chapter Two

'STEP RIGHT UP'

Never before in my life had I ever heard of the Circus. The words that followed made is sound like a dream! In only a few days, there would be bright lights, clowns, tight-rope walkers, trapeze artists, elephants, monkeys, stilt-walkers, and many more performers hustling and bustling through the city streets. MY city streets. The excitement began to rise in my chest. I ran all the way home to beg my parents to take me to the circus. Funny how you can become so excited something that you never knew existed.

I pushed the door open and let it slam behind me, running straight into my Father's office where my mother was sitting, worried about my lone trek and who may have seen me.

"For Heaven's sake boy, what took so long?!" I can still hear my mother's shrill voice questioning me. I held out all of the supplies, "I had to wait a little bit for the medicine." I said quietly, adverting my eyes to the floor.
"Did anyone see your face?" I shook my head and looked to the floor. All I wanted was to be praised to have retrieved everything and all my mother was worried about was her social standing. "Go and get dinner prepared. Your father needs to eat as he is still not feeling well, he will be taking his meal in our room tonight." I caught the words about the circus in my throat as I feared she would just end up scolding me, instead, I nodded, following my mother's orders, I made my way to the kitchen. I had the idea that if I was really good and prepared an extra special dinner for Father, I could bring up going to the circus.

I ran down to the cellar and grabbed chicken, carrots, cabbage, and a few more essentials to make a chicken stew for my father. I recalled reading in a book once that chicken was good for you when you were ill. As I began to cut the vegetables I let my mind wander...

I could see an array of colors. In fact, it was the most color I had ever seen in my life. So many aspects all coming to life all around me. People in bright, sparkly costumes flying and swinging through the air. A woman with three rings around her waist, spinning as she twists her body in all directions. Clowns doing various skits as people watched in awe. I was so entranced in my daydream that I was not paying attention and I ended up adding too much onion in to the stew. The smell made it obvious. I prepared myself for a mental or physical beating when my mother came into taste it, but it never came. I tacked it to her being too tired from being up with my father day and night, she just looked at my and sighed in disappointment. She ended up just putting her hands on her hips. "I'm sorry Mama. My mind began to wander while I was cooking and I accidently added more onion in than I should have. I can remake it."

Mother just shook her head, "No. You can deal with the consequences when your father is feeling better."

"I'm sorry again. It's just I read on the post that the Circus will be here in town in just a few days and I would really like to go...I got caught up in trying to imagine the sorts of things that go on there." My mother looked at me astonished, almost as if I had smacked her across the face. "You're asking to go out in public? Why would you think...." she trailed off, "I'll wear the hat that Elizabeth made me. You've let me go out before, I won't take it off. Honest, I won't." I waited for her to slap me a good one for interrupting. She looked at me as if deep in thought, she grabbed the tray with my father's supper on it. "I'll speak to your father about it. That is not a yes, you're lucky that I'm even considering it." I smiled, "Yes Ma'am. Thank you, I'll do extra chores and keep a close eye on dinner from now on!" I almost could not contain myself as my mother had left the room. She had never shown as much courtesy or even feelings as she did at that moment. I quickly cleaned the kitchen up and ran to my small room feeling like a million bucks. Until...

"Look Peter, it's Freak Face." My brothers had just come in from a game of whatever it is they were playing. "Think he's hiding from his audience?" James shrugged, "Possibly. I haven't seen too many of them stop by recently. Even they are getting tired of looking at him." You see, the children in the area liked to come and stare at me through the window, to get a peek at my head. It's the main reason we got dogs to begin with. I usually tried to stay in my room since it had no windows. "I'm just coming in to get some studies done. " I quickly said and opened a book. I was genuinely surprised when they backed off and let me be.

That evening I was called into my parents' room, my father wanted to speak to me about my stew. "Have a seat, Oscar." He motioned for me to take the seat that was pulled next to the bed as my mother left the room and closed the door behind her. "So, I was told that we had an incident when cooking dinner." I nodded, "You're not in trouble, Son. In fact the soup came out very delicious. Not what I'm used to having but all in all, I wanted to tell you that you did well." I smiled. It was one of the few times in the ten years I had been alive that I ever got any compliments from anyone in my family or anyone at all really, so I appreciated even more when he did. "Mother tells me that you asked to go to the Circus." I nodded again, avoiding my father's eyes, afraid to speak. "Well, how about since you did so well with dinner tonight, even if by accident, and your studies have been remarkable we can go if I can get out of this bed and feel well enough, we can go." I looked up to meet his gaze, he was smiling. I smiled back. "Now, head down to bed, your tutor comes extra early tomorrow." I hopped off of the chair, shook his hand and ran out of the room, as giddy as one could be, passing my mother and siblings in the hallway. "What is Freak Face excited about?" I overheard one brother say to the other. "Who knows? Who cares?" The other responded. I was in such high spirits with the hope and slightest chance that in a matter of a few days, I would be walking among some of the greatest performers of rare and odd talents that the snarky comments of my brothers did not bother me in the slightest.

As if it is any surprise, I did not get much sleep that night. My mind was too excited and kept drifting to images that furthered my insomnia. By the time, I drifted into a decent sleep, I could see the first sign of dawn peeking in under my door. My tutoring session was slightly more challenging due to my exhaustion, but I was still able to pull off the highest of marks before slipping away for a short lived afternoon nap.

I woke to the sound of of my brothers arguing rather loudly with my mother and sister. "Why do we have to go to the stupid circus anyhow?"

"Yea, we don't care about those stupid freaks. What's so special about them anyway?" My mother quickly silenced the shouting, "Hush it up, the both of you! Your father is finally feeling well enough to get up and out of bed and tomorrow we will be going to the circus as a family, whether the two of you like it or not!" Elizabeth followed my mother's words, "Besides, Ozzie never gets to pick where we go."

"Oh, Lizzie, that's not going to help the case at all." My mother groaned.

"He only wants to go because he will fit in with the freaks!" James replied.

I was rather nervous to leave my room for I felt it could spark a scalding from my mother about eavesdropping or a good game of name calling from my brothers, or possibly both. Either way, I was tremendously excited that we were, in fact, going to the circus. I could not contain myself any longer, I made my way out of my room, trying to stay as invisible as possible. I made my way into the kitchen to avoid the conversation still lingering in the front parlor. "Well, Mr. Oscar, good afternoon." Marian, one of our kitchen maids was rolling out dough for biscuits greeted me. "Hello Marian, how are you this fine day? Well I hope."

"Someone is in a good mood. What do we owe this to?" I took a small scrap of bread left over from breakfast. "We are going to the circus tomorrow. I just overheard my mother telling my brothers about it. They don't see too happy." Marian smiled slightly, "I did hear the conversation a little earlier. It sounds like a wonderful time, but be sure to stay close to your parents, those crowds can be somewhat overwhelming."

"Do you need any help?"

"Oh, no Honey. You enjoy your spare time."

I nodded with a smile and made my way out of the kitchen into the backyard. It was my down time and I had an hour or so before I needed to prepare to start dinner.

When I heard the door to the kitchen open and shut behind me, I tensed and readied for a lashing from one or both of my unhappy brothers. I was surprised but relaxed when Elizabeth put her hand on my shoulder. I smiled. She smiled back.

"So, between the three yelling at each other, I am sure you heard that we are going to the circus tomorrow."

"I did. I'm rather excited."

"As well am I." We stood in silence for a few moments before Elizabeth spoke again. "Ozzie, do you think living with the circus would be fun?" I shrugged, popping a piece of bread in my mouth. "I don't know, it seems it would be exciting to say the least. I mean, they get to travel the world all of the time, see different places, meet all kinds of people, be free to do as you feel, learn new things." As I spoke, I could see the expression on Elizabeth's face, she was going to that far off place in her mind she often did when we had our secret picnics. "Oh, Lizzie. Please tell me that you are not thinking of running away with the circus tomorrow!"

"Shh, keep your voice down," she hissed, "I can not stay here anymore, Oz. They are just so horrible to everyone, especially little you. What did you ever do to anyone? All you did was show us how different beauty can be."

"Lizzie, you're my only friend here, my only family. If you leave, there is no hope for me." She stared into me, searching my eyes for any help on her decision. I hoped she got the message that I wanted her to stay.

"You would be my only reason to stay."

"Then stay. You can run away next time when we're both old enough to go." Lizzie looked away from me, she quickly made her way inside. I did not dare follow her to press the subject any further in fear of upsetting my only ally. I was not sure how to handle the news or what to do about it. I ended up making my way inside shortly after Elizabeth to begin dinner preparations. I needed to keep my mind occupied. Marian smiled as I came back in the door. "Mr. Oscar, you should go up and get washed up for dinner."

"Yes, I was just coming in to get cleaned up to prepare the turkey."

"No. No, Sir, you're going to be joining the family at the table tonight. Your mama just came down and told me to set an extra place setting for you." I could not believe what Marian had just said to me. Never before was I ever welcome or allowed to eat in the same room, much less at the same table as my family. I was stunned in time for a moment before Marian rushed me from the kitchen to get ready.

My mother and father were both sitting in the study when I returned, dressed in my best outfit, complete with the hat Elizabeth made for me. They were both speaking in hushed voices and went silent as I walked by the open door. "Well, don't we look handsome," My mother said, "I'm sure by now you have heard that you will be joining us at the dinner table this evening."

"Yes Ma'am. Marian told me, I tried to look my best. I was also made aware that we are going to the circus tomorrow. Elizabeth mentioned it to me a little bit earlier." My father nodded, "Yes, I am feeling much better and in need of some fresh air and entertainment."

"I am both delighted and excited." My mother nodded, "Well, off you go. Your father and I have some business to finish up before supper is served." I ran out of the room as quickly as I could, not sure how to pass the next hour before we were to sit down and eat. I made my way back to the dining room, looking around at the set up. The room was large, a China hutch stood in one corner with dishes only used for special occasions or important visitors. The hutch had been left open, there was a large rectangle table, six chairs in all, two on each side with one at each end. Marian had already set the plates and silverware out. As I ran my hand along the stem of a fork, I felt a shudder come over me, not sure as to why. I shrugged it off as excitement for the next day. I sat in the chair next to the one Lizzie usually occupied. I sat staring at the walls. I had never really noticed the blue pinstripe design that scaled the green walls, but then again, I did not spend too much time in here and when I did, I was pre-occupied with my duties. Dinner was always served promptly at seven thirty every night. I could smell the food Marian was cooking coming through the door that separated the two rooms. I decided to take a peek.

"Mr. Oscar, what are you doing in here? I told you to enjoy your free time."

"I know. It just smelled so wonderful, I could not help myself. I had to peek in."

"Oh, boy. You flatter me." I made it a point to compliment Marian's cooking when I could, she took pride in her meals. I looked forward to trying her food while it was warm and fresh. Marian seemed distracted, almost distant as I stood there watching her finish up dinner. "Are you quite all right?" She looked at me with worry on her face, though she smiled. "I am well, just a little pressured with this meal. It's a very special one and I want to be sure everything is just perfect," she paused a moment, staring at me. She reached out a hand and pulled me to her. The pounding of her heart was almost deafening as she held me. I was a little confused and slightly worried as to why she was so concerned with the food being so on point. "Now, you go out there and you take your place at the table. Dinner will be ready in just a few moments. The family will be starting to gather." All I could do was nod.

Elizabeth was already sitting at the table when I made my way back into the dining room, I avoided making eye contact with her as I took the seat next to her. Mother and Father arrived shortly after, taking their chairs at each end.

"What's HE doing in here?" A few moments later, my brothers appeared, "and at the table. When did we start permitting freaks to eat with us?"

"Both of you WILL mind yourselves. Your father and I have decided that a family dinner before the circus tomorrow is a wonderful idea, there will be no name calling, no taunting, no throwing food, and no kicking each other under the table. Am I clear?" I knew the statement was directed at my brothers but I had never heard the tone my mother had just displayed that I thought it in good taste to acknowledge that I understood as well. "Yes, Ma'am." "Yes Ma'am." My bother, Peter mocked me and stuck his tongue out, "PETER! Did you not just hear your mother?" Father made everyone jump speaking in a stern, yet calm voice. He could be quite intimidating when we was like this. "Sorry, Sir." Peter quickly replied and lowered his eyes to his plate as James snickered. "Same goes for you. I will NOT tolerate you two deliberately disobeying your mother. Is that understood?" Both of my brothers nodded while staring down at their plates. The kitchen door opened as Marian came through with the first course, warm rolls and chicken soup. I ladled my portion after everyone had theirs, mouth watering in excitement to try her fresh cooking. I could not tell what made me happier, the food or the fact that I was actually sitting at the table with my family as a family, finally accepted. I looked around completely aware of the silly grin on my face. "How was everyone's study lessons today?"

"Fine," Elizabeth responded.

"Boring."

"Pointless."

I learned some new things today," I said chimed in after my brothers. "Well, Oscar, that's always a good thing. Education is a very important aspect in life," Father noted, smiling while ignoring the responses of my brothers. I found James and Peter both glaring at me as Marian loaded our plates with beef stew, steamed squash, and roasted potatoes. The smell was Heavenly and the flavor even more so.

"Marian, this meal is just absolutely wonderful," Mother stated. I smiled and nodded in agreement as I looked over at Marian who looked as if she had tears in her eyes. My mother was not a mean woman, she was hard and stern, but not mean. She rarely handed out compliments so they meant a lot more when she did. I was not sure as to why this change in her had come about, but I welcomed it.

"Thank you, Miss. I worked very hard on it." Marian said as she nodded to my mother, "Your kind words are very touching." Marian winked at me. "I have a peach apple cobbler all ready to go when you are ready for dessert." After everyone was finished with their meal, I looked around satisfied. This was how a family should be. "Okay, everyone get washed up and ready for bed. We have a very long day tomorrow." Mother rushed us all out of the dining room. I stopped in the doorway for a moment, not sure how to express my gratitude, "Oscar, don't linger, it's unbecoming."

"I just wanted to say thank you for letting me join you at the table this evening. It was a wonderful time."

"Yes, it was quite lovely, now off to bed." I nodded and made my way to my room, washed myself up a bit and changed into my pajamas. Lying down in bed, too tired to sleep but tried to force myself as I knew I would not get a chance to nap after my tutor had left the next afternoon. I rolled over and squeezed me eyes shut, never in my life could I have expected the events that the next day had in store.

Chapter Three

The next morning, I was woken up by a knock to the front door. Thinking it was my tutor and I was late for my lessons, I jumped up and rushed to get dressed. To my surprise, the guest at the door was not a tutor, but a complete stranger. He was tall, broad shouldered, with dark hair and a mustache that curled into loops at the ends. He had a deep, hearty voice that echoed through the room as he spoke with my mother.

"Yes, do come in. The children should be down at any moment." Mother opened the door fully, welcoming the man into the front parlor. I stared down at them from the top of the stairs, I did not get a great feeling from him. He was not dressed like anyone I had ever seen before. He had a white shirt with a black bow tie hanging loose around his neck, a red sash on the top of his pants which only came down to his knees, and socks that were tucked up underneath. A big red overcoat with black trim slung over his arm with the brightest, most shiny buttons I had ever seen. It was longer in the back than in the front. My mother jumped slightly when she turned to see me there, "Oscar, how many times do I have to tell you? Lingering, especially while gawking at guests in our home is unbecoming."

"My apologies, Ma'am." I said, standing right where I was. "Mr. Colton, this is my youngest child and son, his name is Oscar." She motioned for me to come down, "Oscar, come down." I made my way down the stairs reluctantly. The man smiled at me as he leaned down to stand level with me, "Well, hello there, Oscar. How old are you, Boy?"

"Ten, Sir."

"Ten, eh? That's a good, fun age." He winked as he stood up straight and turned back to my mother. "Looks like a strong little lad."

"Oscar, take your hat off, Mr. Colton was interested in your...head." I hesitated for a moment, I was not sure why this man wanted to look at my head, or how he had even come to find out about it. Once my mother insisted, I took my hat instantly. I figured maybe he was a doctor she had asked to come and take a look. Taking my hat off, the large man gasped. "Well, that is extraordinary. You say he was born with this?" My mother nodded, "Yes, he was born with it. A very rare case, even the doctor had no idea what may have caused it."

Colton stared at me as he spoke to my mother, "So, you were telling me that you are a show folk family. I would lie to hear more about that." My mother motioned for him to follow her into the study, "Most certainly. Just follow me right this way." I was a little put off from the encounter, so I decided to get my stuff and set up for my tutoring lesson which would start any moment.

*　*　*　*　*

Mother and Father finished up with their business meetings, my siblings and I were dressed and ready to go. All of us getting antsy for different reasons.

Finally, we were on our way.

I was so excited, I could barely concentrate on where we were going, the streets twisting and turning. Mother insisted on walking to get fresh air and exercise. I could tell we were getting closer as more and more families were joining us on the trek. The streets were bright even though dusk was upon us. I had a hard time taking it all in, looking around at the banners and signs becoming more prominent and frequent as we got closer. There were so many exhibits and shows to see, I was not sure what I wanted to do first. We stopped at the ticket booth, "Melvin family, we should have 6 tickets on reserve, I believe." The attendant nodded, looking at me with intensity. We took our tickets and passed through the threshold.

It was more amazing than I could have ever imagined, almost like stepping in to a whole different world. Brightly colored banners of red and gold were everywhere, hanging from every post. Red, blue, green, and yellow balloons filled the area, photos of the circus performers hung showing their talents, displayed all over. Lights were everywhere, stands with food that smelled delicious, games, a carousel, and a fun house stood to one side. Exotic animals you could actually ride. I was overwhelmed by the magnificence of it all. "Okay children, what does everyone want to do first?"
"Fun house!" my brothers yelled in unison.
"I would love to see the live mermaid," Elizabeth piped in, they looked at me.
"EVERYTHING!" I shouted excitedly. I could not hold it in any longer, we were really here. We were really at the circus.
"Well, since, there is no way everyone will agree on what to do, how about we split up for the exhibits and side shows then meet back here for the main show later?" Father looked at my mother who just nodded with a shrug. "Maybe Elizabeth can keep an eye on Oscar. If she does not mind?" Elizabeth nodded, "I would be absolutely delighted to take him around. Maybe he and I will have some actual fun." She winked at me.
A band played music, clowns wandered the streets, a man that Elizabeth explained to be a mime put on a silent performance of crying because he was trapped inside a box. "JOIN US NOW! Only ten cents to see the real live mermaid. She will dazzle you with her underwater and above water talents!" Elizabeth and I walked over, holding out our dimes, "No, not for the Melvin children. You enter free of charge." The man ushered us in to the dark area, a large tank standing in the middle of the room. "Lizzie, why do you think he let us in for free?"
"He knew our names, maybe something to do with Mother and Father and their entertainment friends." We watched the mermaid do all kinds of different things in and above the water in her tank. Elizabeth seemed to enjoy it more than

14

anyone. She was entranced by the performance while I tried to figure out the secret behind it. In the area marked exotic, we were able to ride an elephant, a zebra, a camel, and miniature ponies. I had never seen such creatures up close, much less ride them. There was a tiger in a cage, but they were not letting anyone get too close, for good reason I imagine.

We stopped at a food stand that had peanuts, caramel, and candy sticks. Both of got one of everything, I had never had such amazing treats. Time was flying by, it was almost time to go back to meet the family for the main attraction show where all of the side show performers join together to put on one big show. Elizabeth and I finished up our time with games and the fun house. It was remarkable, you step in, the floor would slant one way and then the other, another room it would move back and forth, trying to throw your balance off. A bright light flashed on and off quickly as you stepped into a house of mirrors. The trick to the challenge is to just look for the space where you are not staring back at yourself and go through that one. It's a little disorienting but not completely impossible. I felt like I was being watched the entire time and even as though someone popped up in the reflection behind me for a moment. The feeling kept on through the whole fun house. A smiling Elizabeth was waiting for me outside of the exit when I emerged. "Fun, huh?" I smiled, turning back to look into the house, "Yea, hey do you think they have people in there?"

"What do you mean?"

"I just had the feeling I was being watched the whole time."

"They could possibly have people in there in case someone gets hurt or can't find their way out." I could not shake the feeling that I was still being watched, possibly even followed. "Well, we have time for one more thing before we have to meet up with the rest of the family."

"Want to walk the midway? Maybe play a game?" I suggested.

"Sure, did you have one specifically in mind?"

"Well, I saw one with bottles set up and you throw the ball to try and knock them down. It looked interesting."

"Sure, lead the way." There was a silence between us as we made our way to the game stands. I was never one who was good at sports, yet I really wanted to try something new. I stepped up to the counter, the man just stared at me. "I would like to play the game please." The man scoffed, "Well, little fella, you want to try to knock the bottles over? You can win a prize if you knock all three down."

"Yes, Sir. I would like to try." He laughed as he handed me three balls, taking a deep breath in, I tossed my first one.

Missed.

A little embarrassed, I picked up my second ball and tossed it. Hit but only knocked down two of the three jars.

"Take a moment and breathe, Ozzie. You can do it." Elizabeth encouraged me from the side. I wiped my hands on my pants, still a little embarrassed, a little sweaty, and nervous. An older gentleman came up to take a chance on the game as well. He threw all three of his balls, only to partially knock down the jar towers. "This game is a set up. It is set for people to lose." A little brought down, I did not think I could win the game, I picked up my last ball, gave it my hardest toss I could muster up.

Success.

I hit and knocked down all three jars, no one as surprised as I was. I could not believe what just happened. "WINNER!" The games keeper looked at the man, "Really think it is a set up? This little guy just won."
"Yea Oscar! I told you that you could do it!"
"Okay, Kid. Pick a prize."
I looked around the booth, "Any one I want?" He nodded, "any one you want." I looked back at the different items, a ball, a kite, a musical wind pipe, among a couple of other items. A doll caught my eye. It was a man dressed in a suit with a top hat. I pointed to it, "I would like that one, please." The games keeper handed me the doll, "Congratulations, good job, Kid." I turned to Elizabeth who was beaming ear to ear. "All right Ozzie! Mother and Father are going to be so proud!"
"You think so?" She half smiled, "All that matters is that you're proud of yourself. That was a most lovely throw."

We were the last of the family to show up, Mother and Father did not look pleased in the slightest. "What took you so long? We're going to miss the beginning of the show."
"Oscar won a prize on one of the games."
"What for," James inquired. "Being the ugliest freak here?" Peter quipped.
"PETER!" Father yelled, everyone taken back. "Apologize to your brother."
Peter was silent as he was in just as much shock as the rest of us. He could not get the words to come out. We all stood, staring at the two of them.
"Wha...what did you win, Son?" Mother asked smiling, breaking the silence.
"I won this doll. I knocked over the jar tower with a ball." My voice trembling ever so strongly. "Very good. Now, how about we all get inside. We don't want to miss the opening ceremony." Mother rushed us all inside the large tent, it was almost full of people shoved together on long wooden benches, ready for the main show to start. We found seats together about halfway down the area, the ring was huge, sitting in the middle of the tent, surrounded by the bleachers. A medium sized podium sat in the very middle of it. A long rope stretched between to large, thick posts sat high above the ring. The lights were so bright, they were almost blinding. The noise inside was roaring from the chatter of the spectators. I sat in between Elizabeth and my mother, holding my doll close to me.
My very own first prize.

 The lights dimmed, music began to play. Two clowns came out from opposite sides of the stage facing away from each other, both acting as if they were looking for something. They met in the middle, bumping back to back, both jumping. Turning with their backs to each other to see what they had walked into, finding

16

nothing. They both shrug and then go back to facing the way the came in, finally seeing each other, they both yell. The crowd laughed. The clowns wave, bow and run off stage. That's when I heard a familiar voice, "Ladies and Gentlemen. Boys and Girls. Children of ALL ages, Welcome to the most entertaining show on Earth!" I could not place where I knew the voice from, but it sent a shiver up my spine. The ringmaster took center stage.
He was tall, broad shouldered, he had a red coat trimmed in black. A top hat covering his dark hair, and a mustache that curled into loops at the ends.

Colton.

The weird feeling in the pit of my stomach returned. Something was not right. Something was definitely off. "Prepare to be amazed! We have all kinds of unique creatures, all here to wow you!" He turned as he spoke, "We have clowns, magic, the strongest man alive in the world, a bearded woman, and much much more..." A light came on, directed at the back entrance, "First up, coming to the ring, Rosita, the woman with no bones!" After almost an hour of clowns, elephants, trick ponies, tight-rope walkers, and the real mermaid, the tent went completely dark. IT was pitch black until a giant flame erupted from the center of the stage. A man stepped out from the shadows, a long stick in his hand. He dipped both ends into a small bucket of some kind of liquid and lit them on fire. The crowd 'oohed,' and the crowd 'awed' as he spun them around this way and that, getting faster with each turn, flipping them over his head. A real spectacle! He began to blow the flames high and wide. I was so entranced that I almost did not realize that the screams coming from a few rows over were screams of horror. Before we knew it, the tent ceiling burst into flames. The crowd became hysterical, people screaming, parents grabbing their children, running for any escape they could get to. Animals loose, being chased by the circus performers. "Oscar! Oscar!" I heard Elizabeth screaming my name, just as I turned, I was bumped one way then the other. The last image I saw was Elizabeth's face twisted into a grimace, full of fear.

Darkness took over.

It took me a moment to realize I was being carried with a sack over my head. I kicked and thrashed my arms as hard as I could. I was not sure who had a hold of me, but their grip was too strong for me to get out of. Giving up on my fight, I strained to hear and make out the muffled voices, unsure if someone was rushing me to safety, but why would they be taking me away from my family? Why did Elizabeth have so much fear when she saw who had come up behind me? Finally placed on a soft surface, "Stay here. I promise you will be safe!" A woman's voice, I did not recognize it. The slam and lock of a door. Too scared to move, I left the hood over my head. How did a woman have such a strong grip that I could not even throw her off balance? For what seemed like hours, I sat, not moving wondering where on Earth I had been taken and why. By whom? I heard the door unlock and open. "He has not moved and he still has the hood on."

"Well, get him out." I was led to a dark room, forced down onto a chair, my hood removed.

I was sitting face to face with Mr. Colton.

Chapter Four

"I do apologize for the theatrics, my dear Boy. You haven't been hurt have you?" Too shocked and scared to reply, I just stared at Mr. Colton. "You know, where I am from, when someone speaks to you, you reply."
"No...no Sir. I was not hurt. Where am I?" Colton laughed, "You are with your new family. Welcome to the Circus."
"What about my family?" His smile faded, "Are we not good enough to be your family? Besides, your old family sold you to me. I now own you." Tears stung my eyes, so many questions flooded my mind. Why would my family sell me to some crazy mad man? What had I done? Would I ever see them again? "Why-..."
"Why did they sell you? because, you are a freak and freaks belong here to me, in the circus. To be have an eye kept on them at all times. You will fit right in here. You will be free to do as you please. You also won't have to hide under that hideous hat."
"My sister made that hat for me." The tears finally spilled over. I began to weep. "What ever is the matter? I thought it was every child's dream to run away and join the circus. To see the world, to have no rules. Besides, why would you want to go home to a family that clearly does not want you? Does not love you. Does not appreciate you." Those words hurt, mostly because they were true. I loved my family though, even if they did not love me in return. What will happen to Elizabeth? My sweet Elizabeth. Will my parents tell her the truth or will they take claim that I was kid napped? Lost to the fire, will they put on a charade and pretend to search for me? "My sister loves me," I tried yet failed at sounding brave.
"Be that as it may, Boy, your sister has no way to buy you back nor does she have any clue as to where you are to even try to find you. We will be leaving town tomorrow." Colton stood, looking larger than before. He motioned for me to follow him. He took me to a small tent with a tiny cot sitting in the middle of it. "This is where you will be sleeping." He began to leave, "Oh, I almost forgot," he turned around, pulled out a pair of shackles, "Just in case you decide to try and run home."
"I thought I was free to do as I please here."
"Do not talk back to me. Until I know that I can trust you won't try to run, you will be shackled." He locked one cuff onto my arm and the other to the cot's leg. I was trapped. This man who gave me a weird feeling from the very beginning, who was in my home just that morning talking to my mother. Was this all a set up? The whole dinner and trip, just so this man could purchase me? Was this the reason my parents were being so nice? I did not understand why they would do this to me. I did nothing but help out and try my hardest to please them, I know I was an embarrassment, a monster, an abomination to them, but to go as far as

selling me, to pay someone to kidnap me. I just could not comprehend the whole situation. Tears streamed down my face as I lay down on the cot. I had no clue what I was going to do. I did not want to stay here. I was stuck with this man, a man who buys children, with these strangers. I cried myself to sleep.

I jumped awake early the next morning, the sun barely poking up over the horizon. My sleep had been riddled with nightmares, fear rushing back to me when I was still shackled to a cot in the circus tent. My arm sore from being stuck in the same position for so long. I was not sure what to do, I lie there looking around the tent which would be my new home. I did not want to move, I did not want to be there at all. I just wanted to go home, I was terrified to see what was in store for me ahead.

"So, you're the newest addition huh? What is so special about you?" I turned and was face to face with a young girl, a few years younger than myself. I could do nothing but stare at her. She was very pretty, long flowing blonde hair, bright green eyes, full pink lips. "Well?" She seemed to be annoyed as if my being there was an inconvenience to her. "Oh, sorry. Um, I have a rare deformity on my skull." She reached over and pulled my hat off, she shrank back slightly. "Well, that's not so bad."
"What is this whole 'freak show' thing anyway? Why was I brought here? How does this Mr. Colton guy own me just like that?"
"My name is Catherine," she stared at me. "Oscar," I replied. "Well, Oscar, this whole 'freak show' thing is a part of the circus. They don't really like being called freaks just so you know. Colton buy people on his travels to different countries. As to how he does it, I have no idea. He does not usually purchase children, so I guess most of everyone is actually just hired on." I nodded as I tried to comprehend what she was saying. "Are you part of the show?" Catherine laughed, "No, well yes, well kind of. My mother is Rosita, the Human Rubberband. I will be part of the show soon."
"How did you come to be here?"
"Well, my father abandoned my mother and I, we were pretty poor. My mother was a caretaker in his home and they had an affair. When my father's wife found out that I was indeed his child, she fired my mother and kicked us out of the home. For a while, my father would send us money to help my mother support me and to help us live and mostly to keep quiet about everything. He swore he loved us, but one day it stopped. When my mother asked why, he said his wife forbade him to send anything more. So, we were living in a shelter while my mother did odd jobs to get us by. One day, the circus came through town, my mother knew she had a talent that Colton may have an interest in, so she contacted him. So, now she is Rosita: The Human Rubberband." I nodded in understanding, "And, you have the same talent as she does, I presume?" Catherine lifted one leg up, over and behind her head in one swift move. "Mr. Colton has been trying to talk my mother into letting me in the show, but she told him I had to wait until I was ten years old. Not sure why she picked that age." I shifted on the cot as my arm began to tingle and fall asleep, Catherine looked at the cuff, "Why are you chained to the cot?"

20

"Mr. Colton was worried that I would run away." She pulled a key ring from a small satchel on her side and unlocked the cuffs, "No running," as she took the cuff from around my wrist, "I don't need to be yelled at for setting you free and then losing you."

"I have nowhere to go. Clearly my family does not want me to come home, they sold me to this place."

"This place is not so bad, takes some getting used to, but once you do you will grow pretty fond of it."

She motioned for me to follow her, "Come on, I will show you around a bit, then we can get breakfast and help get everything ready to leave. We will get to travel in the wagons. I will ask my mother if you can ride in ours with us." She smiled, pain filled my heart as my thoughts filled with visions of Elizabeth. I could not help but wonder if I would ever see her again, now hoping that she would make the decision to run away and join the Circus. I followed Catherine down the dirt pathways behind the Circus tents, she pointed out the different ones and what they are used for and who lived in the different personal ones. Some of the Circus performers lived in tents, some in wagons. We came to a medium sized tent that was used as the cafeteria. I could smell whatever was being cooked, it was such a delightful aroma, my stomach began to rumble reminding me that I had not eaten anything other than the circus treats from the day before. Catherine handed me a plate. There was a long table where the food was spread, all kinds of foods. I had never seen anything like it. We filled our plates with egg, ham, bread, and potatoes. I had enough for a King! We were welcomed to sit at a table with some older kids, most of whom were the games keepers and food vendors who were all telling stories from the night before. Catherine and I seemed to be the youngest members.

"Aye, Oscar, you're a newbie, right?"

"Yes, I was kid...er, brought in last night."

"Welcome. I am Dominic, I run some of the games. You look quite young to be working with the Circus, what is it that you will be doing?"

"Oscar is the newest addition to the sideshow." Glances and a few head nods were all I received as a response. "How old are you, Oscar?"

"Ten. Almost eleven."

"Well, that's cause for a toast. You will be making history as our youngest showman." One kid raised his cup, "Owen, put your cup down," another kid nudged him. "So, what's your deal?"

"Deal?"

"You know, your pull. Why is Colton putting you in the show? Especially so young. Must be pretty spectacular." I looked at Catherine then back to the boys who's eyes were all glued on me, "Go ahead Oscar, don't be ashamed. they have seen all kinds of things here." After a slight hesitation, I removed my hat, revealing the large deformity. "Well, blimey." Owen blurted, nudged again by the kid beside him. "You really hide that well," another kid whose name I did not know said. "I was born with the deformity. My mother and father labeled me a monster, my brothers bullied me and called me a freak, so my sister made the hat for me. I have worn it ever since she gave it to me." A few looked as if they felt sorry for me, others a little amazed. I put my hat back on as we finished the rest of our breakfast in silence.

Catherine knocked twice before pushing the door to her wagon open. Rosita, her mother, was packing some things into a trunk. "Hello Mother. I would like to introduce you to Oscar, he's the boy Mr. Colton brought in last night." Rosita looked me up and down, smiling. "Hello Oscar, welcome. I am Rosita. I hope Catherine has been on her best behavior and manners in showing you around." She glanced over at her daughter as she said this. "Oh yes Ma'am, she is. If it were not for her, I'd still be shackled to a cot." Rosita looked back at me with a sudden snap of her head. "Shackled to a cot?"
"Yes, he had Oscar handcuffed to a cot in the center tent, Mother. I let him free not too long ago. We got some breakfast, toured around, met some of the other boys, and came here." Rosita nodded at Catherine's words without taking her eyes off of me. "I apologize for the way Mr. Colton welcomed you. That is not how we act here. I will have to speak to him." She had an accent, different than Catherine's. I had heard it before but I could not place it. "Mother, I was hoping that Oscar could ride along in our wagon when we leave today."
"I will talk to Colton about it, he may already have a place him. Why don't you see if Martha needs any help packing? I'm almost done here." Catherine smiled, "Thank you, Mother." She made her way out of the wagon, pulling me by the arm behind her. "Nice to meet you, Ma'am." The words were barely finished when the door closed, "Who is Martha?"
"Martha is the Bearded Lady. Her and my mother have been friends for a long time. We help her with packing and moving because she has a hard time moving around." We came to a stop in front of a grand tent, "Martha, it's Catherine. Are you here?" The tent flap opened, a stout woman with graying hair and a full beard, not much taller than me stood before us. "Good morning children. How are you this fine day?" Catherine followed her into the tent, "We are well, how are you? Mother sent us to see if you needed help." Martha had a slight limp as she made her way over to a large, cushy chair that looked mighty comfortable. "This must be our new arrival I have heard so much about. What's your name, Son?" Martha finally got a good look at me, I was a little taken back at her calling me son. I rather enjoyed it. "I'm Oscar."
"And, how old are you, Oscar?"
"Ten, almost eleven," Martha looked at Catherine who gave a slight nod. "Well, quite the youngin' are we?" She smiled, "I'm not really needing anymore help, but you two are welcome to stay and keep an old lady company for a while. Maybe Oscar can tell us about himself." She sat back, offering me some candied peanuts, they were delicious. Sweet with a hint of salt. "All right, Oscar, tell us about you."
"Well, Ma'am, I'm ten going on eleven. Sorry, I already told you that."
"S'ok. Continue my boy."
"I'm the son of two entertainers, the are very well known. They think I am a monster."

"Why do they think you're a monster?" She repositioned herself in her chair, "Well, I was born with a deformity," I took my hat off, "They said if anyone ever saw me the family would be ruined. They were not very nice to me. They sold me to the Circus." Martha stared at me for a moment. "It's for the best, Boy. You don't want to be around people like that. No one should be mistreated for what they look like. It was a blessing in disguise, you're here now with people who understand and will accept you." She smiled at me with a wink.

"Thank you, Ma'am."

"One thing, you call me Martha, not Ma'am."

I nodded, smiling back at her. "Feel free to come visit me anytime, but you two better run along." Martha handed me the bag of candied peanuts, "I see you may like these as much as I do."

"Thank you!" I took the bag as Catherine and I made our way out of the tent. "So, what do we need to do to help?"

"We may just go help out at taking the games down and packing stuff up. We could ask Mr. Colton what needs to be done." I hesitated at moving forward, "That guy scares me. Can we not do that?"

"He's not so bad, he just wants to be respected."

"How does he think respect would come from being scared. I would imagine that would make someone hate him." Catherine shrugged, "I guess it has a different outcome for different people." We walked in silence until we came to the man show tent, not a place I was fond of being around. "How long does it usually take to get everything taken down and ready to leave?"

"Usually it's done overnight, within a few hours, but Mr. Colton gave everyone a little break due to the fire." Catherine nudged me along, "I know what we can do." I followed her around the tent, to the side and down a small path to a large tent set off at a distance. I was absolutely amazed when we walked in. She led me to the livestock tent, full of the horses, elephants, tigers, camels, a lion, and a bear. "We can help heard the animals into the traveling crates."

"Um, crates? They travel in crates?"

"Well, not exactly. They go onto the train cars." Catherine picked up two sets of reins, and opened the gate to the camels. "So, we're going to lead them to the train?" She nodded, "All by ourselves?" Another nod. "Are you sure this is a good idea? These animals are gigantic and we are not." Catherine laughed, "The animals are trained, you just lead them and they follow."

"But, they don't know me. I am not moving the lion or the bear by the way." I took the reins that Catherine handed to me. Nervously, I began walking behind her towards the train with the camel following me. The animal was huge compared to me and much stronger. I felt like I was being pushed more than I was leading the animal. Catherine would glance behind to check on me every few feet to make sure all was going okay.

As we approached the train, I tripped and fell. Startling the camel, losing my grip on the reins. He took off at full speed.

"CATHERINE!" I yelled from the ground, "The camel got loose! " She turned, pushed her camel into the train and slammed the door behind it. We both took off after the animal running free, "Oscar, you run to the left, I will run to the right, steer him my way." I ran as fast as I could in the direction Catherine told me to. Terrified the animal get away worse, trample one of us if we got too close. The camel saw me and turned towards Catherine who froze as the large animal ran towards her. "Catherine, move! Just get out of its way!" I thrashed my arms wildly but it seemed as if she could not see me. A loud pop rang throughout the air. Catherine snapped out of her shock and we both fell to the ground, as did the camel. I covered my head as I heard voices approaching. "Check the children, check the camel. Get them all back to the tents," Large hands grabbed me, stood me up on my feet. "You okay, Boy?" Thomas, the strong man was facing me. "Ye...yes sir," my voice stammered. "Is Catherine okay?" he turned me around and began pushing me towards the tents, "You should not have done that." "Catherine! Where is she?" Rosita ran up to us, I pointed to where she stood. "She is fine." Rosita looked at Thomas then back at me, she hesitated for a moment, "Take it easy on him." In a split second, she was gone, running to Catherine, leaving me to wonder what she meant by those words.

Thomas continued to push me towards the tents until we reached a large red and yellow wagon. The door opened, I was pushed inside. Once again, face to face with a very angry Mr. Colton.

Chapter Five

My heart pounded in my chest. I knew I was in a heap of trouble. Mr. Colton was visibly infuriated, he had not said a word though I could feel the anger radiating around the wagon.

It must have been his own personal living quarters. There were copies of posters from the side show performers all autographed around the walls, random sized jars with different oddities inside sat on the shelves, I pulled my eyes away when I came to one that looked like it was full of tongues, my stomach slightly turned. A small table sat to the side covered in papers, clothing strewn here and there, no organization in the place at all.

"Do you have anything to say for yourself, Boy?" I was too terrified to speak, I had no answer for what happened. "WELL?" Colton yelled, slamming his clenched fists onto the table. The wagon shaking making me jump, "I'm sorry, Sir. Catherine told me it would be easy, I did not want to move the animals on our own."

"So, you are saying that it was all Catherine's fault?"

"No, no Sir, it was both of us, but I was just trying to help. I meant no harm at all." I tried my best to hold back the tears that were stinging the back of my eyes, but fear made it difficult. "Why on Earth would you think that two CHILDREN could move my animals all by themselves? I had to tranquilize my camel! He could have run off or worse, KILLED someone." He grabbed me by the shoulders and began to push me through the wagon. I almost fought against him but felt it would be better if I just let him lead me wherever he was taking me.

In the back room of his wagon, I came face to face with a cage just big enough for me to fit inside. He stopped, I did not dare turn around. Then came the worst pain I had ever experienced across my back, pain so bad it knocked the air right out of my lungs. Another painful whip, finally a third. I fell over, I could feel blood trickling down my back. I knew I would soon lose consciousness. "You will learn obedience as I teach it to you," he kicked me into the cage and locked it behind me. "At least you did not scream." He glared at me through the bars, "Now, you will stay in there until I let you out. No more mishaps." He walked back up to the front of the wagon, muttering to himself. I held on as long as I could but finally descended into darkness.

I stirred a little in my sleep, my back sore, my head groggy. Finally, I realized I had been moved, I was outside. There was an odd smell almost like a grassy smell, "Oscar, meet Tyrant. Our lovely tiger." Colton had put me in the tiger's cage. I had a large animal that could take me out in one swipe staring me face to face, I tried to hold myself together, my chest was tight. I could not breathe, I had no idea what to do. The feline made his way towards me, moving slowly from left to right as if he was stalking his prey. I felt the tears welling up, I wanted to scream but was too terrified that it would startle the tiger. I had not a clue as to where to go, no sudden movements I had read. No noise, keep everything within eye view. "See, my boy. This is what you get when you cross me. I do not play games around here. You will learn respect for me, as Tyrant here has. I give one command and he takes your little overgrown head clean off. "Please, Mr. Colton, let me out of here," I begged calmly. "I am sorry I let the camel loose, I tried my best. I really did."

"Oh, now you take responsibility for your actions? When just a moment earlier, you were blaming Catherine."

"I did not blame her, I just wanted you to know that I did not want to move the animals, we were both just trying to help." Colton lifted his arm and brought it down with one swift motion, Tyrant let out a deafening roar in my face causing me to put my hands over my ears and cover myself. "COLTON! WHAT ON EARTH?" I looked over to see Martha coming in to the tent where we were, "Get that poor boy out of there." Colton's expression turned to one of angry confusion. "Excuse me, Martha but I am teaching the boy a lesson." She stared at him coldly. "I do not give a flying hell what you are doing, let him out of there." Colton stared at her for a few moments and then let me out of the cage. Tyrant yawned and laid down, "You know that mangy cat would not hurt the boy anyway."

"Oh, but the fear has been put into him. He now knows." I once again passed out from the fear and exhaustion of the incident.

I woke to a pounding on the front door of the wagon, unsure of how much time had passed. The door swung open, "Well, Rosita. How lovely it is to see you."

"Hello Colton," the door closing behind her.

"What do I owe this visit?"

"Where is Oscar?"

"You mean the mongrel who just caused my men to shoot one of my animals? He has been handled." I so badly wanted to make noise or call to Rosita but I knew it would bring on more punishment. "That camel was tranquilized and will be just fine, besides, the children were just trying to help. Catherine said he did not want to do it to begin with."

"Rosita, our deal is you can take care of Catherine as you see fit, you stay out of the way I handle my business and how I take care of my people here." I heard Rosita sigh, "At least let him ride to the next town in my wagon with Catherine and I." Mr. Colton scoffed at her, "The boy needs to learn a lesson, not be rewarded for bad behavior." His voice began to rise, "Bad behavior? It was a simple accident that could have happened to anyone. He is just a child, he does not need to be punished, he needs to be disciplined in a proper manner."

"Are you questioning my methods of discipline?"

"You know very well that is not what I am doing. I am simply pointing out that he is a child, the youngest one you have ever brought on board with us, and in such a way. He is probably traumatized as it is. I'm just asking that you have some compassion for him."

"Compassion? You are asking me to show weakness! What kind of message does that send to him? To the rest of them?"

"The message that you are not a twisted monster. The message that you understand things happen that are out of our control. He most likely needs to be cleaned up and tended to." There was a slight pause in the conversation, then movement towards where I was. I closed my eyes and pretended to be asleep. Jumping at the loud crash against the cage, "Hey, you little mongrel, get up!" I backed myself to the far end of the cage, away from Colton's reach. My back throbbed from the touch, Colton and Rosita were staring in at me, their expressions could not have been more opposite of each other's. Rosita's one of caring and worry, Colton's of anger and hate.

"You locked him in a cage? Colton, my Lord." He leaned down and unlocked the cage door, I pushed myself further back as he reached in to grab me. "Come on, you are going with Rosita, don't be a nuisance."

"Colton, stop. Let me get him out." Rosita leaned down, ""Do not be afraid. You will be fine with me. We are going to go back to my wagon and get you cleaned up. You will be able to with Catherine on the way to the next town," putting her hand out, I was hesitant to take it too quickly. I did not want Colton to be come even more angry with me, I slowly moved forward. Rosita smiled, "That's it, there we are. Come on." I crawled towards her, taking her hand. She pulled me out of the cage, gently into her arms. I winced at the touch on my back, she turned me around. "Colton, what in the world?" She looked at him, disbelief in her eyes. "I told you he needs to learn to obey."

"As I told you, he is a child, only ten years old. He is not one of your animals you have here that only knows better when you hit them."

"Do not question me again. The only reason I am letting you take him is because I do not want to have him here to keep tabs on him. He is now under your care and supervision. Do not disappoint me." Rosita motioned for me to go with her, "Come Oscar, let's go." She took my hand keeping her eyes on Colton, and led me out the door, letting it slam behind us.

"I am very sorry at how Colton handled this. I do not know what has gotten into him, he has never been this way. I feel like all I have done is apologize for him," Rosita stood behind where I was lying down. She had taken off my shirt to examine the wounds on my back, preparing to clean them out. "Do not apologize for him, he is not worth it." Catherine was staring at me from a chair to my right, "I am also sorry for getting you in trouble. I am to blame and he should not have done this to you. You did not deserve such a thing."

"Catherine," Rosita finished the sentence in a language I could not understand, her accent becoming more prominent. "But Mother, it is true. Mr. Colton should not have whipped him for this accident."

"Is his first or last name Colton?" I asked, realizing that everyone just called him Colton or Mr. Colton.

Catherine shrugged, "No one knows. He is a very mysterious man. Even people who have known him and have been here for years have always just called him Colton."

"Okay Oscar," Rosita stepped up to the table next to me, "This may sting, let me know if the pain becomes too much." I braced myself, tiny shocks went through my body as Rosita began cleaning the wounds on my back. After the first one, she paused. "Let's take a short break before we do the next one," my breathing was ragged, "Thank you, Rosita. For being so kind and for getting me out of that cage."

"You are very welcome, you did not deserve to be in there, and I want the both of you to stay in this wagon until we get to the next town. Colton is not happy that Oscar is with us. You need to rest once we get all of these wounds cleaned out and taken care of."

"Yes Ma'am." I braced myself for the next round of cleaning. My back was on fire for the next few hours but I was more than grateful to be in a safe environment, knowing that I needed to be careful in the future to avoid any more whippings, but also knowing that most likely would not be possible. Mr. Colton was a very scary man ready to punish anyone the moment they make a mistake. I closed my eyes and let myself wander to sleep. I awoke to Catherine offering me lunch, "We have begun out trek to York now, Mother says we should eat and get settled in, it's a decent ride." She handed me a plate with roast beef, vegetables, and a roll. "How is your back feeling?"

"It is still sore, expect it to be for a few days." Taking a big bite of roast beef.

"So, you keep saying you are almost eleven. When is your birthday exactly?"

"I'm not sure of the day. I just know it is around this time of year."

"You do not know your birthday?"

"My family was not very nice to me, I mean, they SOLD me to a complete psychopath. I just remember that is a day in September." Catherine nodded, "Well, why don't you just pick a day and make it your birthday. Then you have your very own day that is all yours." Catherine's idea seemed silly, but started to make sense once I gave it a little more thought. Why couldn't I pick my own day? If I was not sure of my birthday and I would never know it, what was stopping me? "I like that idea. Now to try to pick a day. Don't want to give it too much thought, but make sure it represents me." Catherine nodded, "How about something in the middle?"

"Maybe around the fifteenth? That is the exact middle."

"The fifteenth it is." I had no idea what day it was, but not wanting to look ridiculous in front of Catherine, I figured I would check later or wait until she mentioned it. I was going to be eleven years old, normal children would be worried about grades, I now had to worry about a man who could lash me at any time for any reason. I needed to figure out how to continue my education, I was not intending to stay in the circus for the rest of my life. Maybe there would be libraries in the cities we would visit, I could buy books they were getting rid of and I could check out the old shops in town as well. "Um, Catherine, does Mr. Colton pay the performers in the circus?"

"Yes, I do not think it is very much since he provides meals and a place to live. The performers get to keep any money that is given to them by visitors though." That information gave me an idea, I would do the shows that Colton wanted me to do and maybe extra stuff to earn a little more. I was determined to save up some money and get away. I told Catherine that I really needed to rest, I felt tired and my back was bothering me, I honestly just wanted to be alone with my thoughts. I needed to figure out a plan. "I will go help Mother, if you need anything for your back, let us know, we will help you." She smiled and took the plates. I needed to get a plan together. I lied down to get my thoughts about me. Eventually, I drifted off to sleep.

I saw Elizabeth. She was standing in the hallway outside the den of our family home, I tried to call out to her but no sound came from my mouth. She just stood there, staring into nothingness. She could not see me and tears were running down her cheeks. She was crying. Could it be because I was missing or had something else happened? Elizabeth had something clutched tightly to her but I could not make out what it was. She turned, looking behind her as if someone had beckoned her, someone she could hear. Taking a look back at the door, I heard her say, "Goodbye Ozzie." She disappeared down the hallway.

I jumped awake, covered in sweat, burning up. "Are you okay?" I blinked to adjust my eyes, Rosita was sitting on the chair, staring at me. "Just a dream, about my sister." She nodded with a look of sympathy on her face. "How are you feeling? You look a bit flushed."
"I'm hot, my back hurts, but other than that, I guess I am okay."
"Well, get some more rest, we will be in York soon."
I did not really want to fall back to sleep, dreaming about Elizabeth again was not at the top of my agenda, mostly because she looked like she was in so much pain. "Miss Rosita, do you have any books?"
"Um, nothing I think that you would be very interested in. Catherine is not an avid reader, so nothing really for your age range. It is all mostly medical books and such."
"That is quite all right, I prefer to read educational books, I just do not want to fall asleep and have the dream of my sister again." Nodding, she handed me a book called Introduction to Anatomy. I was a book on where everything in the body is located and how it works. "I have a bookshelf full, I took them when I was asked to leave Catherine's father's home. I wanted to be a nurse. I joined the circus so we had a place to live and I could make money while studying, but I just ended up not having the time to dedicate and moving around so much, it would be hard to get stable work to get my foot in somewhere. I hoped that Catherine would take an interest, but she has taken an obsession to the show."
"My parents were show folk. I would always study a lot of the business aspect because I knew they would never let me take over the acting side of things, if they were to let me take over at all."
"Yet, here you are. Going to be a showman yourself." Rosita tried to give me an encouraging smile, :My parents were very vain. They said looks were the first and most important thing to have to be a performer. They said if anyone were to see me and knew that I was their child, they would be ruined." Rosita frowned, "That is not true at all. We all have our very own special things that make us who we are." She rubbed my head and moved to the back of the wagon, "Now, I should get some work done, enjoy your book." I nodded with a slight smile and began to read.

Chapter Six

By the time we arrived in York, I had finished two books on anatomy and one book on psychology. I have always took pride in being a fast reader and learner. I retained what I read the first time I would read it. Rosita looked through the window of the wagon, "Well, we have arrived. York, such a place." I looked at Catherine, "What does she mean by that?" Catherine shrugged, "No idea." Rosita turned to us, "I guess we should go see what Colton wants everyone to help out with." The three of us made out way out of the wagon, meeting up with a small group also on their way to get their assignments for the day.

"Well, hello there Oscar, how was your ride over?" I turned to see Martha coming up behind me. "It was okay, I did a lot of reading, very educational."

"I am very surprised a boy your age enjoys reading."

"I love it, one of m favorite ways to pass the time."

"Well, I have plenty of books if you ever want to take a gander at them. Always a blessing to have children want to educate themselves."

"With all due respect, Martha, I do not plan on being in the circus forever, I think I may look into the medical field." Martha smiled, "And, why not?" We continued the rest of our walk to meet up with Colton, a number of thoughts running through my head.

"Most of you know your assignments, a lot of you have you own areas to get set up. I will be assigning some of you to walk through the city to make our presence known. Thomas, today you will be walking the prepared advertisement to the town's paper office. You will have Oscar, our newest arrival joining you. Oscar, leave your hat here. I want those town folk to see that head of yours." Rosita looked uncomfortable with my assignment, I was not sure if I should be worried. Thomas was the Strong Man, he seemed nice enough. His act consisted of bending objects that were deemed almost impossible, he broke cement bricks with his bare hands, lifted a variety of items that no other man could ever dream of even moving in the slightest. I tried to give a confident smile to Rosita to help ease her mind a bit but even my nerves were going completely crazy.

Thomas made his way over to me, "I guess we should get going, we need to have the ad in by a specific time to be printed for tomorrow." I was surprised to hear an American accent from Thomas. I surely thought he would be European. His whole demeanor threw me off, he was a younger guy, possibly not even twenty years old, decently tall, broad shouldered, arms larger than anyone's I had ever seen before. He looked intimidating from afar but his voice was calm and steady, mild and not intrusive in the slightest. Rosita came over to us, "I will hold your hat for you in the wagon. I do with he would have kept you here on the grounds." "Thank you. It's okay though, it will give me a chance to get some sight seeing in." Rosita smiled and took my hat. Thomas and I took towards the town, not too far from where we would be setting up camp. "So, where are you from? Your accent sounds American." Thomas nodded, "You would be correct, I am from New York."

"How did you come to be so far from home? With the circus?"

"Well, Mr. Colton was visiting my hometown, I was out in a bar having a drink when a fight broke out. I tried to break it up only to do more damage had I just left it alone and waited for police to arrive. That is when Colton approached me, he offered me a job in return to helping me get out of the charges."

"How long have you known about your strength capabilities?"

"I have been stronger than most all my life, no one really knows how. My muscles tend to advance and strengthen more rapidly than others." As we walked into the more populated streets in the town, I could feel people staring at us, a few even crossed the street as to not have to walk by us. "Do not let it bother you, Kid. These same people will be at the shows trying to get as close as they can in just a few days." We stopped outside of the editorial office when two men came up to us. "What do we have here? Looks like the Circus is in town," one of them laughed to the other. "Yea, by the looks of these two, I would bet my left arm on it." Thomas reached out his hand, "No need to lose body parts over it," he had a couple of tickets in his hand, "Here. Take these free tickets and see if you can find some pretty gals to come along with you." The two men looked surprised, "Ha, freaks!" They exclaimed, one grabbed the tickets from Thomas and they both ran. "Wow. That was kind of cool."

"I am not big on fighting, it is a waste of time. You have the those kind of people in every town. They think they are better than you because you are different, but the moment you call them out on it, they run. Most people will just walk away once they see they are not getting a rise, and some will push a little harder, but stand your ground. Do not let people like that get to you." Thomas and I proceeded in to the editorial office.

"Well well well, Thomas. What a nice surprise. Is is that time of year again already?" A woman behind the counter was remarkably beautiful. She resembled Catherine slightly with her golden hair and green eyes, she was petite with a warm and welcoming smile. "Hello, Iris. We are back around. How are things here? Are you holding down the fort?"

"Things here are just wonderful, thanks for asking. Papa has brought in all kinds of new business and advertisers," she looked to me, "Who is this little fella?" Iris smiled as she looked at me, I could feel my cheeks burning. I became speechless. "This is Oscar, he is our newest addition to the show. You can say hello, Miss Iris is one of the nicest girls I have ever met."

"Hello," is all I could manage to say. Iris was the very first person I had met that did not wince or shrink back when meeting me. "Hi Oscar, I'm Iris. You seem pretty young to be running away and joining the circus."

"My mother and father sold me to Mr. Colton."

"Oh, dear me. I am terribly sorry, I did not mean any offense. Don't you worry though, they are a good close family. They will take care of you pretty well." Iris turned to Thomas with a look of slight embarrassment on her face, "Did you have the advertisement? I can get it on the press for tomorrow morning's edition,"

Thomas handed the paper to Iris, "Don't you forget to save me a seat on opening day." She smiled and Thomas and winked at me, "Of course, can not wait to see your smiling face there." Thomas smiled at Iris as we made our way out of the office. "I think she likes you."

"Iris? Nah, we have known each other since I came to the Circus. Her father owns the editorial office and she has helped him out after her mother passed away. She is just polite because we bring in so much business."

Two days later, it was opening day. Everyone working so hard to get all of the tents, booths, and stands set up. I did a great job of staying out of trouble, but this would be the day I ruined that streak. It was in Colton's own tent that I refused to take the stage. I was not ready for it just yet, I was not ready for the world to see me and to mock me. I needed to have a plan, a draw. I did not want to just go and stand on a stage with people staring at me. Everyone else had some kind of wow factor to their performance. "But, Mr. Colton, Sir. No one is going to be amazed at a young kid with a large head deformity standing on a stage doing nothing. I would really like to have a show prepared, to draw in the crowds." He pushed me back against the wall by me neck, "Look Boy. I will tell you this once and only once so you better listen up. You do not say no to me. I own you. No one says no to me. You worry about getting ready and going out in to that ring tonight. I will worry about pulling the crowds in. Understand?!"

I was dropped to the floor, gasping for breath. "Yes, Sir." When I stood up, Colton grabbed my shirt, ripping the sleeves off, pulling it open, buttons flying all over the tent. "This will help you look roughed up. You will be going on after Rosita tonight, so go get ready. Try not to disappoint me." I walked out of the tent, once again terrified of Mr. Colton. Upset with myself for being so stupid and talking back to him, knowing he was not going to listen to me. Rosita was stretching before the show, dressed in a blue leotard with sparkly rhinestones all over the front. "What happened to your shirt?"

"Colton was trying to rough me up for my performance, he thinks this will help me look the part. Not sure what he is going to do to me this evening," Rosita shook her head, "He really has become a difficult man." I shrugged, "He has me up after you."

"I am not surprised, he always put his new acts after me. I guess I am not shocking enough to end on."

"He is ending the show with me?"

"He always does with new acts."

"How does that make any sense? I do not even have a real act, it will just be me up there, standing and doing nothing." Rosita continued her stretches, "I am sure he has been working on some kind of angle for you, Oscar, let us hope it is nothing too crazy. Colton would never let the show turn to a bust."

I watched from backstage, all of the acts going up. The crows oohing here and aahing there, thunderous applause during the big finales, gasps at surprising or nerve racking moments. Iris watched Thomas from her seat in the front row with a smile on her face and a gleam in her eye. Once Rosita took her place, I noticed

Colton making a bee line straight for me, he grabbed me by the arm and forced me into a cage.

"I thought I was up next!"

"You are. Here is your bit. This will be how we introduce you, try to look rabid and feral. I want them to be afraid of you, to fear you. No one knows you were born with this deformity. You could be a flesh eating maniac for all they know."

"So, you put me in a cage?"

"Yes Boy. So when you break out, they will all be terrified. I will shackle you and save the day." Hid plan sounded completely ridiculous to me, not sure how people would believe a small ten year old boy such as myself would be a feral flesh eating cannibal, let alone fear me, all due to the deformity on my head. My nerves began to kick in when Rosita was nearing the end of her act, I ended up vomiting all over myself, "Well, that will definitely help with the disgust factor. You will be cleaning that up after the show." He pushed his way back through the tent, "Rosita, the Human Rubberband. Isn't she amazing?" He waited for the crowd to silence before speaking again, "Now, Ladies and Gentlemen, boys, girls, children of all ages young and old. We have the final act of the evening coming up next. I found this young specimen on one of my recent trip to the jungle. His parents are rumored to have abandoned him, they found him to be a monster. His condition is hideously disturbing." The curtain opened and the bright spotlight found its way to me. I was blind for a moment, I threw myself backward as the cage was pushed forward. I tried to move around like a terrified yet aggressive child would. The crowd was in a stunned hush. I threw myself against the side of my cage, one woman screamed, another fainted. I laughed to myself at how ridiculous this all seemed. I could tell my shoulder would be bruised, but if the act went well, it was worth it. "Now, I ask that you all be silent as I try to coax him out of the cage so you can get a better look. He is known to eat human flesh. The deformity on his head is said to come from a witch doctor's revenge for eating his daughter. He would forever have a second head growing out of his own as a reminder." Looking at Mr. Colton absolutely confused as he opened the cage door, "Come on out and say 'hello' to the people. They are here just to see you." I moved slowly towards Colton, trying to look as feral as I could, as wild as any child abandoned in the jungle would. He 'coaxed' me out, a dance like movement between us, I hesitated and made my move towards the crowd, screams of horror rang out, the crack of a whip pierced the air and my back stung as it had just a few days before. Looks of terror were displayed on the faces in the crowd. I stopped in my tracks, falling to my knees. Colton snapped a shackle around my ankle. All I could see at that moment was Iris's smile had faded. I was barely holding on to consciousness. My back was in so much pain, I wanted to give into the darkness. This was one part of the act I do not think I would ever get used to. After a few moments, Colton finished his set through it was all a blur and gargled to me. I succumbed to the black hole that awaited me.

The dream came as soon as my eyes closed.

I was in my family home once again. Elizabeth was standing in the main parlor, crying. She was holding onto something so tightly the muscles in her arms were trembling. I tried to call out to her, to let her know that I was alive, that she should join me in the circus, but to my dismay, once again no sound would come. She just stood staring into thin air, with a far off look and tears falling down her cheeks. She did not even care to wipe them away. She turned slightly as if someone called her to them. I finally saw what she was holding.

The doll. The one I had won during our trip to the Circus.

She stood and began to run through the hall, I ran after, following her through the home. The house seemed to change, it turned dark, only a light coming from a room at the end of the hall, the room that was my own. Elizabeth had disappeared. I was alone. I made my way down the hall to the room, pushing the door open wide. I jumped when I saw the man in the room. Looking more like a shadow, but a familiar presence. He was holding a bloody knife, I began to scream.

Flying out of my dream, screaming. Rosita, Catherine, and Martha all stood around me. "I can not believe he just left him here like this. What if he had gone into shock?" Iris stood not too far from me in Thomas's arms, her cheeks wet, eyes red. "I had another nightmare." Rosita nodded, "You need to rest, Oscar. We will get you cleaned up and back to the wagon." I drifted back off as someone who I imagined to be Thomas carefully lifted me and began to carry me.

At that point, I had no idea the extent in which the nightmares would take over my life.

34

Chapter Seven

Five years had passed. I was still the last act that Colton had brought into the Circus. At sixteen years old, I had grown into a young man. I hit a growth spurt which put me around five foot seven, a little stocky from all of the work I did putting up and tearing down the circus. My voice had deepened and my mind flourished. I was still furthering my education, and had grown close to Rosita, Catherine, and Martha. We all kept an eye out for each other and took care of one another. We were family. Before I made the decision to move into my own tent to give Rosita and Catherine who was now fourteen their own space and privacy. I felt guilty waking them up every night with my nightmares, they claimed not to mind and that it did not bother them but being a male, I felt it was time to stop intruding on them. Catherine and I had began to spend a lot of time together on our off days, touring different cities and I still rode with them to the next stops. I had read every book in Rosita's personal collection, some of them multiple times. I began helping when the animals would take ill or if someone was injured. Colton still disliked me to an extreme extent for some reason. I can only imagine it had to do with my act growing in such popularity, he could not keep up with me. Everyone wanted to see the cursed cannibal, he who had been punished by a witch doctor for making dinner of his daughter. It was worth the lashings I endured every night. I had stashed away quite the chunk of money, not anywhere near what I needed to go out on my own, away from the circus, but I was getting there. Catherine was growing into a beautiful young lady and I feared the feelings I had started to develop for her. I had come to accept that she would never be interested in me, Martha was a major help with my studies. She was once a school teacher before joining the circus and would tutor me during our breakfast every morning. Iris and Thomas finally admitted their feelings for each other, she began visiting and traveling with us when she could get the time approved by her father to leave the editorial office. I remember another time I once again made a dire mistake and took advice from her. I do not blame her in the slightest for trying to help me, even though she has apologized many times for the instance. You see, as I got older the nightmares became more intense. I began to miss my family, well, my sister Elizabeth and I feared something was wrong. I confided in Iris my nightmares, how it was in my home, she was in random places, holding the doll and crying. The man who was just a shadow holding a bloody knife, how no sound would come out when I called to her. How Elizabeth would be completely gone when I reached the room with that man. Iris explained that she felt my dreams were telling me that I was worried that Elizabeth was still hurting over the loss of me. That I left and she did not know if I was okay or not. She suggested that I go down and send a telegram. Just a simple message to let her know I was alive and well. I agreed it was a good idea, she and I took off towards the local office. An older gentleman behind the counter stood when he saw us enter. He was pleasant, took my message, and sent it. I was nervous the whole time, the feeling of being watched that never left lingered, and I could not believe I would actually be sending a message to Elizabeth. "Do you have a name and town to send it to?"

"Yes, Elizabeth Melvin in London. Just a simple to the point, 'I am alive and well, Oscar.'" The man nodded, "Very simple. Very to the point." I paid the due, Iris and I were on our way back to the Circus grounds. When we showed up, Colton was waiting for us, well more so he was waiting for me. He smacked the side of my head so hard my ears rang, I stumbled but managed to keep upright. Iris screamed for him to stop as he began to pound on me, a crowd starting to form. "Did you think I would not find out, Boy?" Everyone too afraid to do anything just stared at us, I covered my face as he kept hitting me, aiming more so for my back. "Find what out? What did I do?"

"Do not try to play me for a fool! You sent a telegram to your family! Why on Earth would you do that? After they sold you to me, they gave you up, they did not want an embarrassment like you around, a monster plaguing their family. After five years of taking care of you, giving you a place to stay, feeding you, paying you, this is how you treat me. After five years, you think they give any kind of care about you?"

"I only sent a message to my sister," I cried." She did care about me, she was the only one who did. I just wanted to let her know that I was alive, I told her nothing else." Colton halted his attack. "If she cared so much, then how come she never tried to find you? How come you are still here? She never cared, she just felt sorry for you." He shoved me to the ground and stormed off. Iris ran over to me, "Are you all right?" I pushed myself up, "I'm fine."

"Do not listen to him Oscar, He is just trying to upset you. He does not know anything about your family or how they feel about you." I shrugged, "Maybe he is right. How come Elizabeth did not come to look for me?"

"Ozzie, a little girl is not going to be able to look for her missing brother on her own that easily. With us leaving that very next day, how do we know she did not go back to the grounds?" I turned to see Catherine beside me, "Elizabeth used to call me Ozzie." Catherine blushed, "I'm sorry, I did not know that. I can stop if you want."

"No, I like it," I smiled, Catherine smiled back. "Okay then, I shall keep calling you that." She rested her head on my shoulder, "Do you want to get out and see the city tomorrow?"

"Sure, that would be wonderful." Iris smiled, "Do you mind if Thomas and I tag along? Getting out and about sounds like a lovely idea." Catherine shook her head, "Not at all, it will be good for us all. We will make a day of it." Iris perked up, "I'm so very sorry that I gave you the idea to send that telegram, I really did not know he would get so angry."

"He just feels that he owns most of his performers and workers. He feels that since he paid for a lot of them, he has claim."

"You can not own people, most stay because they fear him." I shook my head, "Well, I guess I better go get cleaned up," I said goodbye to the ladies and headed to the tent that I had recently made my home.

The next morning, I awoke to Catherine standing by my cot. Staring at me, making me jump. "Did I give you a fright?" She giggled, "No more than usual." I winked as she playfully punched me on my arm, "Whoa there, Tiger. Don't want to classify you with Colton."
"Get dressed," rolling her eyes, "Let's go have an adventure."
"Are Thomas and Iris ready to go?"
"They are packing some food for a picnic," She grabbed a shirt from my night table and threw it at me. "Besides a picnic, any idea on what you want to see today?" Catherine shook her head, "Nothing specific really, "We want to walk around, look at the city. The architecture here is stunning."
"Stunning," I mocked with a laugh. "Oh hush. I will leave without you."
"No you won't."
"Okay, maybe I won't but would you hurry on already!"

A few hours of walking around the city, we found a park not too far from the circus grounds. The four of use sat down to our picnic. The day had been beautiful. It was just the four of us, looking at the sights in peace, talking about general life topics, not stressing over the smallest move. It was one of the best days I had in a while, it really took my mind off of everything that had been happening. "The weather is just absolutely amazing today."
"How come we never go to cities that have beaches? That would be a grand time." Iris chimed.
"Maybe Colton is worried we would all disappear and never come back, besides there are not too many places around that have beaches and the space to put on the show." Thomas retorted.
"Is that truth or is that what Colton has used an excuse not to go to the beach areas?" Iris answered,
"Maybe he just doesn't look good in a bathing suit." We all laughed, "We will just have to take the time to go visit whenever we are close."
"I honestly don't want to go back. It has been so nice today, I don't want to ruin it." Catherine stated, we all agreed. It had been a wonderful day, it was a pity that we had to go back to the circus and have it ruined. I was not looking forward to my act later. It was starting to take its toll on me, my back was scarred, my head body was bruised from slamming myself around the cage. The only positive note was that I no longer blacked out after the performances.
Catherine looked over at me, "What are you thinking about?"
"Just the show. My act, it's been the same for the past five years. I know there really is not much you can do with it, but it just feels stagnant." Catherine nodded, "You could always be a rubber band and wow people with stretching further than they can," She nudged me, smiling. "If I wanted to put people to sleep, I would take you up on that."
"Ha, rude." She laughed then leaned over and kissed me on the cheek. "We should probably head back to get ready. for the show. We don't want to anger the beast." We all laughed as we packed up the leftovers from our picnic.

As we walked back, Iris and Thomas were further ahead of Catherine and I, talking about the weather again. "So, Oscar, are you still thinking about leaving the circus?"

"Well, I know I do not want to be here forever. I was thinking about maybe going into the medical field when I am old enough. This world is not for me."

"But, it is for me?" Catherine asked, "That is not what I am saying. If you feel this life is for you, then it is. If you want to do something else, by all means, do it. I never wanted to be here, I did not want to be a part of this show. It was forced upon me. I have enjoyed my time with you, I love that you and your mother have taken me in and we have become close. Other than that, there is nothing here for me." She looked a little hurt by the words I had just said, "I want you to know that you have made my time here better. I have not had a good run if you have not noticed." She smiled slightly. "Well, I guess I can accept that then. I do not want to stay here forever either, but I can not leave my mother." I nodded, "I understand that. How about when we are both ready to move on, we make a pact and we go, taking her with us. Would she come?" Catherine shrugged, "She feels she has locker herself here and tied herself down, but I think it is more that she knows she has a life here and is stable. But, if we all leave together, the three of us can make a life for us somewhere else."

"Where would you want to go?" She took my hand as we walked, "I have always been fond of London," I tensed a little, "London, really?"

"Oh, Ozzie. I am so sorry. I completely spaced, it would not have to be London." I smiled, "If London is where you want to go, London is where we will go. I will follow you wherever." She stopped and turned to face me, "Really?"

"Really. I have loved you since the first day I met you. I felt the greatest connection the first time we spoke and it has only grown since then. I never thought you would ever feel the same way." Catherine giggled, "Well, I do." She leaned up and kissed me, on the lips. My very first kiss ever, with the very first girl I had ever had feelings for. It was one of the most amazing moments I had ever experienced in my life.

I was floating in the clouds when we returned to the Circus, though the mood was somber. Not one was out socializing like they usually do before a show. In fact, no one was out at all, it was eerily quiet, "What do you think is going on? Everyone should be getting ready for their shows." Catherine stated, "It's so quiet," Iris added. We continued to walk through the circus grounds, looking around for anyone to ask the details. "I am going to go find Mother. I will meet up with you later." I nodded and squeezed Catherine's hand before she ran off to her wagon. "This is really crazy." I looked at Thomas, "I am going to go find Colton, see if I can get the story. Iris, stay with Oscar." Thomas kissed her forehead and went in the opposite direction Catherine had gone. Iris looked at me, worry in her eyes. "This is a bit unsettling. It is always so lively here. What do you think happened?"

"No idea," I shrugged, "I have never seen it like this, I hope nothing too serious." Iris moved closer to me as we continued through the walkways, both of on edge.

A loud crack came from somewhere on the grounds, "What was that?" Iris squealed, "I don't know, it came from that way."

"Should we go see what it was or should we wait? It could be something dangerous. Maybe we should wait until Thomas gets back, and Catherine. To be sure they are okay first." Iris was becoming hysterical. "It is going to be okay, Iris. Don't let yourself get worked up, we can sit here and wait for them if you feel more comfortable." She nodded, "I do."

"Then that is what we will do, let's sit over here on the bench."

It was not long before Thomas and Catherine came running back to where we had decided to wait, "Ozzie, it is so horrible! The tiger got free during the set up and attacked John. He is in the tent now, they are not sure if he is going to make it. Colton canceled the show for tonight. He sent everyone to their tents and wagons. Come quick, Mother said to see if you can help. They can not get a hold of the doctor." The four of us ran to the tent where John was as fast as we could, Colton was sitting next to the bench he was lying on. "Oscar, can you help?" Rosita ran to me, "I don't know, I have never done anything like this before. He is going to need stitches, do we have the materials? Has anything been injured internally?" "We do not know the full extent of injuries, the tiger bit down pretty hard, but we do not believe that anything has been punctured inside, we have cleaned the wounds, the bleeding has slowed." I took a look at John's wounds, they were deep but did not look too fatal. I took a deep breath, "I can try." I made the crowd leave the tent so I could concentrate, Rosita and Catherine helped with supplies as I cleaned the wounds again then doing my best at stitching his wounds closed. "I can not make any guarantees on anything, but I feel he will be okay." I said to Colton and headed to my tent, Catherine following close behind me.

Rosita came to my tent a little over an hour later, "May I enter?"

"Of course you may. Please, tell me how John is doing." I urged her. "He is doing well, he is stable. His breathing is back to normal, pulse is strong. He told me to tell you thank you, you saved his life. Colton is also very grateful."

"I did not do it for Colton. I hope he knows that."

"Even if you did not do it for him, he is thankful, and you should accept that. You did a wonderful thing tonight, Oscar. The entire camp is talking about how amazing it was." I nodded, "I am going to head back to the wagon. Catherine, do not stay out too late. I foresee an early morning." Catherine nodded, "Yes, Mother. I won't be too much longer. I just want to make sure Ozzie is okay before I come back."

"Goodnight Oscar, I will see you in the morning."

"Goodnight, and Rosita, I am sorry for the way I spoke to you. My nerves are on edge right now."

"Do not apologize to me, Son. Emotions are high in everyone, get some rest," she said and exited the tent.

"Are you okay? Really okay?" Catherine put her hand on my back, I took it in my hand. "I just, tonight really sunk it in for me that this is not where I belong. It only made me want to leave sooner rather than later." I turned, unable to look her in the eyes, fearing that she would not be ready. "Ozzie, if you are ready then so am I, but, do you think we can make it on our own? Even with Mother, I just don't know how we will be able to do it."

"On our next trip to London, let's at least look and see what is there for us." She nodded, "Okay. It is still a few months away, we can save up a little more and talk to Mother about our plan."

"Do you think she will go with us?"

"I hope so. I could never imagine being without her." I kissed Catherine on the forehead. "Do you want me to walk you to your wagon?" She shook her head, "It's not far, I need the time alone to think. Goodnight Oscar." She kissed my cheek softly and left.

Chapter Eight

The years went by so quickly. Catherine and I had saved up enough money to leave the Circus about five years after the incident with the tiger. Against Colton's wishes, Rosita came with us. Things were going well, almost too well.

We found a small home in the Whitechapel area of London, Catherine took a job at the local newspaper while Rosita and I worked in the medical center not too far away. Rosita was nervous about starting a new life and was worried that she would be imposing on our life together at first but ended up giving in after Catherine told her we would not leave unless she came with us, not wanting to hold us back and keep us in a lifestyle we did not want. I think she was more worried about getting back into the real world after spending so many years in the same routine. Catherine and I married a few years after we left and were working on starting our own family. Life was getting on the track that I had dreamed about as a child. It was not that easy to leave the Circus, Colton was not happy that his most popular act was turning his back on him, as he put it, while taking one of his longest running performers.

I became a successful medical assistant quickly, the surgeons were very impressed as they had never seen anyone with my ability to learn and perform duties in such a manner. I began to take on my own patients and help out with surgeries so I could log the hours needed in order to become a practicing doctor. Working long hours took a toll on my home life, but we were content as any young couple could be. It was not until one night when I had stayed late at the hospital to keep an eye on a young woman who had her appendix removed that the real strain began on out marriage. Her name was Eliza, which reminded me of my sister. I sat and talked to her about many different things to keep her comfortable while in recovery. Her surgery went a bit rocky and we were monitoring her vitals throughout the night. She was a sweet, young girl with aspirations of becoming a writer. She had grown up living with only her father and brother as her mother had passed away during childbirth. She had so much zest for life and told me she had planned to leave for America the following month. I assured her that the surgery would not upset those plans. I started to wonder what it would be like to visit America, I had heard many different things about the country and thought maybe we could take a trip one day.

Catherine was visibly upset when I walked in the door that night, I tried to be as quiet as I could so not to wake her as she had early mornings at the news office. She was waiting up for me, eyes puffy and red, cheeks tear stained. I was not sure why she was so upset, we had a good life.

"It looks as if we need to talk, my Love." Sniffling, she looked at me, "Will talking help? I feel as if our life has been turned upside down. Why have you been staying so late at the office these past few evenings? Are you actually staying to work or is there something you should tell me?" I was surprised beyond belief. How could Catherine, the first and only girl I have ever loved in such a way think I could ever be doing anything to wrong her? Sure, I had wonderful conversation with Eliza. Sure, I stayed late at work when I did not have to, but only because I felt I could give her the best care. "Catherine, how could you think I would do anything to hurt you in any way?"

"You took this job so we could become more independent. You promised you would be home at night so we could have dinners together as a family. You promised we would not live under someone else's rule."

"Yes, and I have stood by all of those promises except for the past few nights. I have had a patient at the office who had a shaky surgery and felt that I was the best person to look over her in case something should happen."

"Her?" Catherine asked, looking hurt and confused.

"Yes, a young girl named Eliza. She had an appendectomy two days ago, it did not go as planned so we had to perform some new techniques. It is not anything more than that. We are not living under someone else's rule, once I can save up to open my own practice, I promise, I will be home nights. You have to understand though, medical practitioners are on call around the clock."

"Would you be taking so much interest if this was a male patient?"

"Of course. I stand by my work and my career, Catherine. I can not push someone aside. Besides, Eliza is recovering nicely and should be leaving the center within the next few days."

I had no idea that Catherine had a jealous streak. I wonder how long she had been holding all of these emotions and thoughts inside. I hoped that she was always honest with me and would tell me if something bothered her. I knew that things were going a little too perfectly and I now was worried that this was going to be the start of major issues between us. "Why have you not brought this up to me before? I have stayed late at the center to study and learn new material in the past. Maybe not as much as recently. I am doing this for us."

"I have not brought it up because I did not want to upset you, I do not want this for us. I want us to be a family."

"We are a family. If I do not perfect my skills, I will never be able to have my own office and patients. Then, where do we stand? Me always working in the medical center as a practitioner. I want to be a surgeon. I want to run my own place." Catherine shook her head and sighed, "This is why I kept this to myself. I did not think it would do any good. I spoke to Mother, she thinks that maybe she and I should take some time to travel."

"You mean without me..." Catherine turned from me, "Yes, just her and I. I think it will be good, you can spend time perfecting your skills and I can work more on my writing and possibly come back to a career with the newspaper."

"Do you really think that you will still have a job after just deciding that you need to take time for yourself and just up and leave?" Catherine just stared at me, I wish I knew what was running through her mind. "This isn't working, Oscar.

You know this, I know this." I sat down with my head in my hands, "If something is not working, you do not just set it aside and leave it, you work on it, you fix the problems that are there." A blank stare was her response. "I do not know what to tell you. I have tried and tried, I kept it to myself thinking that it would pass. Now, even sitting here trying to talk to you about it, I get an excuse and the response of it is going to stay how it is until you can open your own practice. How is this fair to me? How would it be fair if I was with child?" I looked up, "Are you with child?"

"I have not received the official word yet." I stood, a little more excited than I should have been for an unofficial announcement, but we had been trying so hard to have a child.

"Why did you not tell me? Why did you not have me examine you?"

"I think some things still need to be kept private until they are worth mentioning." I took a step towards Catherine who flinched backward, "Do you not want me to come near you for some reason?"

"Oscar, this does not change my decision to take time apart. This is not something I am tell you to mend and make things better. I fear this news will only make things more stressful and pressing." I sighed, "This is joyous news if it to be true, how can you say this will not make things better?"

"Because, things will not change. You said yourself that you will be working as much as you can at the center until you can move on from it, which when will that be? A year? Five years?" I began to wonder why if Catherine were with child she would be wanting to leave so quickly, it occurred to me that something was off, not just my late night hours at work. She had always been supportive and encouraging of my work ethic. Her stance did not seem genuine, something was off. "So, if I promise to not stay late anymore, not even while Eliza is in my care. To come home every night for dinner, that will suffice? You will stay and not take the time away?" I started to become suspicious of Catherine, "This time away is needed and it has been decided. Mother and I will be leaving in just a few days." I nodded, stepping back, looking at Catherine who would not look me in the eye. "So, there is nothing I can do to make you stay?" She shook her head, and gave a simple "No."

"Catherine, if I may be so brave, if you are with child, why would you be leaving? Is it because it is not mine?" Her eyes flashed of fear, "How DARE you? Are you accusing me of being with someone other than you?" Her voice was shrill but calm and collected, "Well, it just does not make any sense. Why would a woman who could possibly be with child who may not the happiest at home be willing to leave so quickly without even trying to give me a chance to work on the circumstances you have now brought to my attention that you are unhappy with?"

Silence.

All of the color had drained from Catherine's face, she was breathing heavily and seemed to be sweating. This confirmed my realization. She was in fact with child, a child that was not mine. Catherine sat down and began to cry, "I'm so sorry, Ozzie. I did not mean for this to happen. I love you, I really do."

"Do not call me that." I could not get my thoughts about me. How could she have done this to me? How could she have betrayed me so? I had not done anything to purposely hurt her, everything I was doing was to make life better for us, to move us up in the ranks of society, and to get us to a better place. I grabbed my medical bag and made my way to the door, "When you go, do not come back. I never want to hear from you again." I slammed the door behind me and started towards the medical center, figured it would be best to keep my mind occupied and there were plenty of things to be done around there.

It was an eerily quiet night, there was no one out and about like there usually was. The streets were empty, it was as if the entire world had disappeared. I was alone with my thoughts. I was brought to face the reality of Catherine's words, my love for her had quickly turned into feelings of hatred, feelings of confusion, and feelings of anger. I could feel a bubble of rage boiling inside me, I needed an outlet. I noticed a small figure up ahead, stumbling around as if they had possibly had too much to drink, maybe lost on these dark alleyway streets. I decided to follow them for a little entertainment. As I came up behind the person, I noticed it was a woman. Small in stature, older than I. She had dark hair that was starting to grey, a lopsided smile, and dark eyes. She was having obvious trouble walking, "May I lend you a hand, Ma'am?"
"Oh! You gave me a fright, Boy. What are you doing walking around in the middle of the night?"
"I could ask the same of you, do you need some help?" I held my arm out, she took it. "Where abouts can I drop you at home?" I asked as we began to walk with no general purpose or direction. "Trying to get into me home, are we? Cheeky boy. Would you like to have a grand time with me, is that what this is all about?"
"No Ma'am, just trying to be a decent citizen and doing a good deed for someone who needs help." She pulled away from me, "Aye, who said I needed any help? I was just on me way home, I never said anything about needing help." Her words slurred and she wavered slightly as she spoke, I took a step closer, "I did not mean to offend, Ma'am, I..."
"My name is Annie, not Ma'am." Of course it was, I almost laughed at the coincidence of the situation, and for a brief moment, I pondered if this was my mother that I had been torn from so many years ago. This Annie did not seem as if she was old enough to be Annie Melvin. She pressed herself closer to me, "Or maybe you want to have a good way with me and you are just using the decent citizen act. You do not have to be coy with me, Boy. You could just ask." I was repulsed by her actions, I was not interested in the slightest of having a grand time or a good way and I did not like her being this close to me. I took all of the rage I had been holding against Catherine, Colton, and my family who abandoned me.

I pushed her backwards, she stumbled and fell, "Oy, what is this about? You should never 'it a lady!" She tried to get up, I pushed her down, grabbed the small knife I had in my pocket. I opened it up and began to stab, I could not stop myself. It took Annie a moment to realize what was happening, most likely due to the amount of alcohol, she was feeling no pain at first, "HELP! HELP ME! He's trying to kill me!" Once I felt there was a possibility of getting caught, I grabbed the bag I had dropped and I ran. I ran in the direction of the medical center as I was heading before. Voices began to get closer behind me, running towards her screams.

Chapter Nine

I pushed the door to the medical center open, running in and making my way straight for the lavatory to clean up any possible blood I had on me. My pulse was racing, heart pounding, such a rush it was. I took a moment to pull myself together and as calmly as I could, I made my way out into the hallway looking around for anyone who may be doing their nightly rounds. There was no one in sight so I headed to the nurse's station to check in, just like I would any other time. "Oh, Dr. Melvin, I did not expect to see you here at this time. Were you called in?" I smiled at the young nurse behind the desk, "No, I had a not so great night and needed to get out of the house, I figured I would come by, check on Eliza, and get some much needed charts done." She smiled with a slight nod, "One reason I am glad to work overnights, keeps my mind occupied." She handed me Eliza's paperwork, "She has been up and walking around tonight, she says she feels ready to head home."

"Well, that is a good sign. I will take a peek in and see if she is still awake, maybe we can look into discharging her tomorrow." I took the paperwork and headed towards the Recovery wing, pushing the door open as I looked over the attending doctor's notes. "Doctor Melvin, it's a little late for you to be here, is it not?" I looked over to see Eliza sitting in bed, reading by candlelight. "Well, you are still awake. I was just doing some late night rounds, decided to come in and get some work done." She marked the page in her book and closed it, setting it on the table beside her bed. "You work a lot," I laughed, "I am trying to open my own practice one day, so I plan to get in as many working hours as I can, learn as much as it takes to make that dream a reality."

"Have to respect a man who works hard for what he wants." I smiled, "I guess so. Some people do not see it in such a manner though." Her expression turned into a perplexed one, I just nodded it off.

"I hear you are ready to go home. I think we may be able to work that out tomorrow, I will double check with Doctor Marzel, but I do not see it being any kind of an issue." The door to the recovery wing flew open, "Doctor Melvin, we need you right away! A patient has just been brought in." My heart and my stomach felt as if they had switched places, could it be the woman that I had just encountered?

As not to look suspicious, I followed the nurse to the operating room right away. My suspicions were spot on for the second time this evening, Annie Millwood lie on the table in front of me. I had no idea what to do, I was the reason she was here and now I had to decide to help save her life. This could be the biggest step forward in life if I could get her to a full recovery. "Nurse, prep the patient for surgery. Female patient, looks to be in her mid to late thirties, multiple stab wounds to the lower torso and legs, I can not be sure what she was stabbed with.

Looks like possibly a small knife of some kind." Everyone jumped as Annie's eyes flew open and she gave out a scream, "Let's get her sedated shall we?" The nurse gave a nervous smile and began anesthesia. Once she was under, I went to work immediately. Checking each wound for any kind of shards possibly left from the knife that stood in my pocket at that very moment. It was a long process to get all of the wounds closed, though there was no major internal organ damage. With my nerves on edge, it was slightly difficult to keep my hands from shaking throughout the surgery, but as I finished, the nurses congratulated me on a successful job well done. I left the room quickly after giving the nurse orders to have Annie under close supervision for the rest of the night, that I would be staying in the doctor's quarters in case any problems were to arise. Once I was in a private area, I let my emotions get the best of me. I began to hyperventilate, my body shaking and my palms sweating. I had no idea what I was going to do, what if Annie recognized me when she woke up? What would I do if she went to the police and told them I was the one who attacked her? So many scenarios ran wild through my mind, I splashed some cold water on my face and began to change into something I could be more comfortable to lay down and rest in. All of the staff of the medical center left clothing and some personal items in case we ended up having to stay longer than planned, never know when an emergency or a disaster could happen. It was best to be prepared. I lay down on the bed, closed my eyes, and let myself drift into a light sleep.

Elizabeth stood before me, I could not see where we were but it was nowhere familiar to me. She had not plagued my dreams in so long, it was most welcoming for her return. I reached out but she backed away from me. "Oscar, how could you?" I knew I was dreaming but it felt so wonderful to hear her voice again, if only in my head. "You hurt that woman."
"But then I saved her life, Lizzie." I reached out again, she backed away further.
"You should not have done that."

I opened my eyes, daylight was coming in through the windows of the small room. Elizabeth had never spoken to me in my dreams before, I was confused as to what she was referring to when she said I should not have done that. Was she warning me to something that would be happening? The knock at the door startled me, I stood and put a coat on. It was most likely something to do with Annie. "Doctor Melvin?" A young inspector stood in the doorway before me, "Yes, may I help you?" He took his hat off, "Yes, Sir. I was wondering if you could sit and give me some details on the woman who was brought in last night. Annie Millwood." "Um, sure. I guess I can give you as much information as I have." I stepped out, closing the door behind me and led the inspector to a small office we used for consultations and meetings with patients before and after procedures. "Have a seat, Inspector. Would you like some coffee or tea?" I motioned to the chair as I took my own, "No. Thank you, that will not be necessary, this will not take up too much of your time. I know you are a busy man." I nodded, "Sometimes," giving a slight chuckle to try to not seem as if I was hiding anything. "The victim was brought in around what time last night?"

47

"Let me think, I had just arrived not too long before. I was checking on a patient we had here. I would say it was around eleven thirty or so."

"You say you had just arrived soon before?" My heart skipped a beat, "Yes. I - yes, I had just come back after running home to check on my wife. You see, she is with child, but we have a patient here who had a not so easy surgery about a week ago and I wanted to be here just in case."

"Well, good thing you were. You are a real hero." I smiled, "I am just doing my job." The inspector wrote down a few notes, "How many stab wounds would you say the victim had?"

"Well, it is hard to say, some of them were close together on the body so it was a little difficult to decipher where one may have ended and another one had began. I would say around twenty-five to thirty, give or take." His eyes widened slightly at my count, "Whew, that is a bit of an attack. I am surprised she even held on to make it to the center here." He stood, "Well, that is all I have for now. If I need anything else, I guess I will contact you." I stood, nodding, "Yes, please do, if there is anything I can do."

"I would say just keep being in the right place at the right time."

"I shall try." I followed the inspector out of the office and through the hospital, showing him to the front door.

I went back inside to check on Annie, saying hello to Eliza on my through. Annie was lying in bed awake when I came in. I was nervous as to how the encounter would play out, but when I stepped up next to her, she just gave me a slight smile. "Morning Doctor."

"Good Morning, Miss Millwood. How are we feeling?"

"Call me Annie, I am feeling as well as I can considering the circumstances, I guess." I smiled down at her, "You did very well with the surgery, there were no complications. There was no internal organ damage, a little bit of tissue and nerve damage, but once you are feeling up to it we can go into a little more extent. I just need to check on the wounds to make sure the stitches are holding up." She waved her hand slightly as if to say 'go ahead.' I pulled the sheet back, her lower torso was covered in bright red wounds. There would be major scarring, both sides of this were my works of art. "The good news is, the stitches are holding up nicely. The bad news is I did my best but I am certain there will be major scars." Annie laughed, "Oh, Doctor, at my age, it really does not matter. I am alive, that is all that counts for right now. I am not worried about the scars."

"Try to get some rest, I will have one of the nurses come in later to clean you up a little bit and to get you some lunch." I pulled the divider closed and started on my walk back out to the main hall, "Doctor Melvin," Eliza motioned for me to stop by her bed, "Is she going to be okay? Will she survive?" She whispered the questions, "She has some extensive scarring that will happen but I am optimistic on her survival. She is through the worst of it, now it is just healing." She nodded, "She was talking in her sleep last night. She does not know the man nor does she remember what he looks. It is a scary idea to think that there is a man out on the loose running around stabbing women for no reason." I nodded, "Yes, yes it is."

"Maybe someone saw what happened and will come forward," Eliza smiled as I tried to keep composed, "That would be ideal. Now, let's see if we can get you out of here, if you are ready."

"As ready as I will ever be," she laughed. I stood up, heading for the nurse's station to get the paperwork ready for Eliza's departure. It was a bittersweet moment as I rather enjoyed having her around yet I was happy she was fully recovered and ready to go back into the world to pursue her dreams of traveling and writing. It would be back to the normal grind after she left. "I have been thinking about possibly writing about my time here at the medical center. Not sure what I would do with it, maybe just keep it for my portfolio so when I finally muster up the courage to look for writing jobs, I will have it on hand." I smiled, making my way down the hallway, "Nurse, we are going to be setting Miss Eliza free today," I said with a light chuckle, "I think she has endured enough of us here. Can you get the paperwork all set up and I will sign off on it in just a moment, please?"

"Sure thing, Doctor Melvin."

I slipped away to get my wits about me. Between the ordeal with Annie and the dreams of Elizabeth starting again, I felt I could lose my mind at any moment. Eliza's idea that someone could have seen what happened and come forward did not occur to me. Once Annie did not recognize me, I really thought I was going to get away with it. There I was thinking it could all come crashing down. There was a knock on the door, opening it, to find a young girl standing in front of me. "Are you Oscar Melvin?" I nodded, "My name is Annabelle. I am the daughter of a man you knew as Colton." I stared at her, not sure what to say, not sure as to why she was here. "May I come in?" I snapped out of my stupor, "Yes, of course. Please...sorry, I just have not heard that name is quite a long time." I opened the door wide and let her into the office, motioning for her to take a seat. "Can I get you anything?"

"No thank you. This will not take long at all." I sat down opposite the desk from her, "How can I help you?" She was a pretty girl, short, thin with dark hair and dark eyes. She resembled Colton but you could tell she mostly took her mother's looks. "Well, my father recently passed away,"

"I am sorry to hear that. He was a decent man." She smiled slightly, "You are being kind, I appreciate that, but my father was no decent man. He was a wretched fool who did not know how to treat anyone." I had no words, "I know that he was paid to kidnap you from your family and that you were a part of his sideshow. You traveled with him for quite some time and left on not great terms." She pulled a large envelope out of the bag she had around her shoulder, "I was going through his estate and cleaning out his home as well as his wagon at the Circus. I came across some things I feel you should see. I am not sure how this will affect you or if it is my place to even be here right now, but I think it will do my own mind good that I did my part. I felt you should see how he felt about you and to tell you that he left you the Circus." I was taken back by her words, I was not sure how to react. I loathed the Circus, I loathed everything about it. When I left, I left for good. I did not want to own it. I took the envelope, torn between

looking at it with Annabelle sitting with me or leaving it for when she departed. "You were his favorite performer, he treasured your presence. You were his most popular and he felt you had grown into a fine young man." She looked around the office, "If he could see where you were now, he would probably feel even more proud. He thought of you as one of his own. Well, if you decide to read the entries, you will see all of that." I looked at her as she stood up, "I feel you should read over everything there, it may give you some insight as to why he was the way he was." I nodded, standing. "May I ask you something?"
"Sure."
"Was his first or last name Colton?" She laughed, "His first name was Merv."
"I see now why he just went as Colton." She nodded, "Most do."
"My name is Oscar, so I guess I can not poke too much fun." With a slight giggle, she held her hand out, "It was very nice to finally meet you, Doctor Melvin. I had heard so much about you growing up, it was nice to finally put a face to the name." I shook her hand, "I am surprised I have not met you before now, I would have thought you would have been running around the circus with the rest of us."
"My mother was not fond of my father's business. She felt it was cruel to keep people and animals under such an environment." I nodded, "Makes sense." She made her way to the door, "Maybe our paths will cross again, I live in the area." She was gone.

I turned to the nurse, signed off on Eliza's discharge papers, and made my way back to the recovery wing to check on Annie. She was asleep when I arrived. Not wanting to wake her, I decided to head back to the doctor's quarters.

A month or so later, the medical center had been as quiet as my home had been. Catherine and Rosita left right after our last argument, I had not heard from either of them. I did not really expect to. I spent most of my time at the medical center, studying up on new procedures we were coming upon daily. I decided to give the Circus ownership over to Thomas and Iris who were still traveling and performing with it, I felt they were the best choice being there from almost the beginning. They were grateful and it took a load off my mind to know I did something for someone else. Maybe life would move forward and get back to normal for me soon.

Chapter Ten

Once again I was wrong.

The morning of April seventh, I arrived at the medical center, one of the few nights I had not stayed over. I was not happy going to the home that Catherine and I once shared. I was tired of it and thought about putting it on the market.

I stumbled across the morning edition of the Eastern Post, I gripped the newspaper in my hand tightly as I read the headline:

Alleged Fatal Stabbing Case in Whitechapel

It appears the deceased was admitted to the Whitechapel Infirmary suffering from numerous stabs in the legs and lower part of the body. She stated that she had been attacked by a man whom she did not know, and who stabbed her with a clasp knife which he took from his pocket. No one appears to have seen the attack, and as far as at present ascertained there is only the woman's statement to bear out the allegations of an attack, though she had been stabbed can not be denied.

This is how I heard of Annie Millwood's passing. I was not a success. She ended up dying as a result of what I did, now it was a murder investigation and I would most likely be expecting to answer many questions for the police inspector. I was not prepared for this by any means. I thought I was home free. I needed to think of a story quickly. I jumped and almost stumbled down the step when the voice came from behind me, "Good Morning, Doctor Melvin. How are you? Just getting in?" I turned to see not only one but two inspectors coming up the walkway, "Yes, I actually just arrived, what can I do for you gentlemen?"
"We see you have already seen the morning post."
"I have," looking down at the paper in my hand. "We only stopped by to tell you that the coroner has deemed Miss Millwood's death that of natural causes. In his words," he pulled out a notebook, "the victim suffered sudden effusion into the pericardium from the rupture of the left pulmonary artery through ulceration," the notebook closed and was placed back in his pocket. "Well, that takes a big weight off of me, I always feel I try my best for the patients that come to my table and I was slightly worried I had not done enough for her."
"That is the exact reason we stopped by, we wanted to let you know that it was unrelated to her injuries she had sustained last month." I nodded, "Well, as sad as it is that she has passed on, I am slightly relieved it was not due to my hand, if that does not make me sound like a monster."

"Not in the slightest," one inspector said, "I would be delighted to know I did not have a hand in the matter." Said the other. I could not tell if they knew how hard my heart was pounding in my chest, I may not have been the reason she passed away, but I was definitely the reason she was brought in to the center. I was relieved that she would no longer be around to talk in case she finally remembered who had attacked her that night. "Well, gentlemen, if there is nothing else, work calls."
"Of course, Doctor. We will leave you to it. Have a nice day." The inspector tipped his hat, "You as well." I watched them both closely as they made their way down the front walk and out of the gate.

Sitting at my desk in the office, I was not able to focus on my work. All I could think about was Annie Millwood and how things had happened that night, how easy it was to get her to come with me, how easy it was to jam the knife into, how easy it was to get away. That was when I realized what Elizabeth had been trying to tell me in my dreams. I should not have attacked her, because I would come to like it and want to do it again.

Summer had come and gone, late August was here and Autumn was upon us. I stepped out for one of my leisurely strolls around the city to clear my thoughts. It was a quiet night, the streets were pretty empty, everyone either in their respectable homes or out at the less respectable brothels, the dirty places they were. I had my medical supply bag with me as I was out looking for a victim, well not looking but I would not turn one away if they happened upon me. I feel my mind had finally snapped, I was not the man I was before. I did not care about dreams and aspirations, I did not care if women were only doing walking the streets to make due and to get by, to help their families. The sad excuses for human beings needed to be taken care of, to be exterminated. That was the reasoning, as sick and ignorant as it was that Catherine gave me when she finally came clean that the child was not mine. She told me how she was not doing as well at the paper office as she had hoped she would, as she led me to believe and that she turned to prostitution to help get us by. Of course, I did not notice it because I was so caught up in my work, I did not notice her sneaking out of the house, taking customers in the alley outside of our home when she claimed to be running to the cellar. I was blind to it. But now, now I would have my revenge. I would have my revenge on Catherine, on Colton, on my parents, on my siblings. I would have my revenge against anyone who had hurt me. I know that the people I would hurt were not those people, but worthless, grimy, sick, wastes of space that I could take my aggression and rage out against. No one would miss them. No one would care.

It was almost too easy to find an unsuspecting victim, so many of them wandered the streets looking for gentleman callers. Those men are no gentlemen in my eyes, most of them are married with families whom they are out running around on to begin with. She came around the corner as I reached it and bumped right into me,

"Aye, what you doin' out 'ere all lone, Mister?" Why are so many of them drunken fools? Is that how they force themselves to continue doing what they do? "I was looking for you." Her eyes went wide and a smile spread across her face, "You was looking for me?" I nodded, "Yes, what is your name?"

"My name is...well how were you looking for me if you ain't even know my name?"

"It does not matter then." I started to walk by, continue on my way. "Aye, my name is Polly. Polly Ann Nichols." She was shorter than I, could not have been more than five-three, stout, brown eyes and a dark complexion. She was layered in clothing, probably to keep herself warm in the cold. Her eyes were glazed over, I could tell she was not really here. "Polly, eh? That is a beautiful name. What are you doing out here all by yourself?" She giggled, "I was looking for you." She staggered slightly and fell into me. I can not believe men would still have their way with someone like this, easy prostitute or not. "Why don't we take a walk and stretch our legs a little bit, Polly."

"Aye, sounds like a nice plan. I can show you my favorite little corner."

"That would be lovely." She took my left arm in hers, linking them as if we were a happy couple and we began to walk down Buck's Row. I kept my wits about me, keeping an eye out for anyone who may be passing by. The street was completely deserted, I knew if I was going to make my move it would have to be soon and swift. I could not afford any mistakes. "I have a present for you, Polly." She gazed at me, not really able to focus, "For me?" I put my medical bag down, opened it up and pulled out the knife I had hidden away. She could not see that I was holding it, in one quick move, I ran the knife along her throat so that she could not scream, spilling blood, catching it in a glass I brought. Her hands immediately reaching for the open wound, a gurgling sound I had never heard before from her mouth. She tried to speak, tried to run but stumbled, I brought my fist back and let it smash the side of her face. She fell to the ground, I went to work. I sliced her abdomen and ran the knife along a couple of inches. It was slightly dull so I had to use a saw like motion, I made a few more incisions until I heard what sounded like someone coming down stairs close by. I packed my bag and made my move, trying to be as silent as I could and moving in a quick but not attention grabbing manner. As I walked away, I could tell Polly was still breathing.

I arrived home not too long later, it was not far from where I had just struck my second victim. It was such a rush and it was confirmed that I enjoyed this. I really enjoyed it. My adrenaline was on high, I felt like a new man. I knew they would be finding her body soon, did I want to go back and witness the discovery? No, that was too dangerous, if they saw me there they would want to question me. I decided to stay home, I did not even go to the medical center. I wonder who they would call upon to examine the body, if she was alive would they bring her into my office? What if she dies before they get her help? I had so many thoughts floating around my mind, I was not sure what to make of them. I decided to give myself a cleaning up, just in case they came around to call on me.

I woke the next morning for my scheduled duty. I had not dreamt of anything the night before, I fell into darkness and stayed there until I awoke. I splashed some water on my face and grabbed my clothes. I packed my bag and headed out. There was a calm about the morning, I figured there would be a madness, a mass hysteria but there was nothing. I wanted to make a statement with this attack, I wanted people to be scared, to know that there was a murdered loose, and to be afraid it would happen again because it most definitely was going to. I would find and stalk another vile creature of the night and I would do the same to her, maybe even worse. I arrived at the medical center to a welcome from the night nurse. "Still here huh?" She nodded, "We had a visitor last night, he was looking to speak to you but Dr. Odersand took care of it."

"Looking for me? Why would someone come in looking for me?" She shrugged, "There was a murder last night and the inspector wanted your take on it, but the doctor on duty took care of it. He said that he felt you were working a lot and you needed your time to yourself. Nothing major." I nodded, "Is there a report somewhere I can take a look at?" She handed me the file, "It was a pretty cut and dry case, woman was murdered, throat was slit. Well, you will see the details when you look at the file, pretty gruesome." I opened the file, the whole report laid out before me. "I will be in the office if anyone needs me, is Dr. Odersand still here?"

"I believe so, they were trying to find next of kin for the deceased."

"Thank you, Nurse." I picked up my medical bag and headed down the hallway to the doctor's quarters to change and then to find the doctor who handled Polly coming in. I could hear voices coming from the area we took the cadavers after we had examined them, I pushed the door in and poked my head to see who it may be. An older man stood with Dr. Odersand, he was clearly distraught but he did not seem surprised that he was standing next to the body. "Mr. Walker, I am terribly sorry for your loss." The doctor put his hand on the man's shoulder, the man who came down to identify the body of this woman. "I am not surprised by this. Mary Ann was a troubled woman, we had a lot of problems when she lived with me when her husband left her. She was a dissolute drunk who I knew would find a bad end," he looked down to the woman's face, "I do not know who would have done this, she had many friends, I never knew her to have an enemy, even if she was difficult with me." My presence was detected, Doctor Odersand turned towards me, "Well, Doctor Melvin. Good morning, this is Mr. Walker. He came down to identify a corpse that was brought in last night." The man began to cry, "It is such a shame that is what she is now, I am sorry. I wrote her a letter not too long ago, I never heard back. We had a bit of a tiff the last time we spoke, I can not believe I never got to make things proper between us again" Doctor Odersand led the man towards me, "We are the ones who are sorry. Let's go sign off on the identification so we can release the body to you. There is nothing more needed here." I stepped aside to let them pass, once I was alone with Polly's body, I made my way to it, looking it up and down. I pulled the sheet back to examine the wounds, they were messy. Not those that would look like a doctor's, this would not come back on me, unless once again someone had seen me leave the scene. Only time would tell, I did not fear anything being linked to me. I sat down at my

54

desk to go through the report and have my morning tea. The report was short, nothing too advanced really, but I already knew that. I knew everything about the murder, I wonder if I would be questioned. Would they even do an investigation on a prostitute? She did not deserve the attention. I sat back in my chair, I was already gearing up to find another to add to my list.

Chapter Eleven

I went out for my morning coffee and to grab the daily post to see if there had been anything about Mary Ann Nichol's murder, non to my surprise, there was an extensive article related to just that.

A shocking murder was discovered in Whitechapel morning. Shortly before four o'clock Police constable Neil found a woman lying in Buck's row, Thomas street, with her throat cut from ear to ear. The body, which was immediately removed to a mortuary, was also fearfully mutilated. The deceased has been identified as Mary Ann Nicholls, thirty six years of age, who was recently an inmate of Lambeth Workhouse. No clue to the murderer has, however, yet been obtained.

BRUTAL MURDER IN WHITECHAPEL

A murder of the most brutal kind was committed in the neighborhood of Whitechapel in the early hours of yesterday morning, but by whom and with what motive is at present a complete mystery. At a quarter to four o'clock Police constable Neill, 97 J, when in Buck's row, Whitechapel, came upon the body of a woman lying on a part of the footway, and on stooping to raise her up, in the belief that she was intoxicated, he discovered that her throat was cut almost from ear to ear. Assistance was procured, a messenger being sent at once to the station, also a doctor had been called into, where he hastily inspected the body where it lay and pronounced the woman dead. The details of the horror that had been done to the body are not for the faint of heart. The lower part of the woman's body was found to have been horrible mutilated by three or four deep gashes. Any one of the wounds was sufficient to cause death. After the body was removed to the mortuary of the parish in Old Montague street, Whitechapel, steps were taken to secure, if possible, identification, but at first with little prospect of success. The clothing on the body was of a common description. It was discovered that the skirt of one petticoat and the band of another article bore the stencil stamp of Lambeth Workhouse. The only articles in the pockets were a comb and a piece of looking glass. The latter led the police to conclude that the murdered was an inhabitant of one of the numerous lodging houses in the neighborhood. She was turned away from her lodging house on Thursday because she had not the money. She was then the worse for liquor. A woman of the neighborhood saw her later, she told the police - even as late as 2.30 on Friday morning - in Whitechapel road, opposite the Church, and at the corner of Osborn street, and at a quarter to four she was found within 500 yards of the spot murdered. Nicholls left the workhouse to take a situation as servant at Wandsworth common. Her stay there, however, was short. From that time she had been wandering about. She was a married woman, but had been living apart from her husband for some years. Her age was thirty-six, and had been an inmate of Lambeth Workhouse off and on for the past seven years. She was first admitted to the workhouse seven years ago, and from this point seems to have entered upon a downward career.

The matter is being investigated by Detective Inspector Abberline, of Scotland yard, and Inspector Helson, J Division. The latter states that he walked carefully over the ground soon after 8 o'clock in the morning, and beyond the discoloration ordinarily found on pavements, there was no sign of stains. Viewing the spot where the body was found, however, it seems difficult to believe that the woman received her death wounds there. The body must have been nearly drained of blood, but that found in Buck's row was small indeed. The police have no theory with respect to the matter, except that a sort of "High Rip" gang exists in the neighborhood which, "blackmailing" women who frequent the streets, takes vengeance on those who do not find money for them. They base that surmise on the fact that within twelve months two other women have been murdered in the district by almost similar means - one as recently as the 6th of August last - and left in the gutter of the street in the early hours of the morning. The other theory is that the woman whilst undressed was murdered in a house near, her clothes being then huddled on the body, which was afterwards conveyed out to be deposited in the street. Color is lent to this by the small quantity, comparatively, of blood found on the clothes, and by the fact that the clothes are not cut. If the woman was murdered on the spot where the body was found, it is almost impossible to believe that she would not have aroused the neighborhood by her screams, Buck's row being a street tenanted all down one side by a respectable class of people superior to many of the surrounding streets, the other side being a blank wall bounding a warehouse.

Doctor Odersand from the Whitechapel Medical Center was called to the scene to examine the body. He made the statement today - When I arrived at the scene, I took a quick examination of the body. I found that the throat had been cut from ear to ear though there was little blood, her legs were out straight, her head turned slightly to the side. I noticed a crowd had started to form so I ordered the removal of the body to the mortuary, telling the police to send for me again if anything of importance transpired. There was a very small pool of blood in the pathway which had trickled from the wound in the throat, not more than would fill two wine glasses, or half a pint at the outside. At the time I had no idea of the fearful abdominal wounds which had been inflicted upon the body. At half past five I was summoned to the mortuary by the police, and was astonished at finding the other wounds. I have seen many horrible cases, but never such a brutal affair as this. From the nature of the cuts on the throat it is probable that they were inflicted with the left hand. There is mark at the point of the jaw on the right side of the deceased woman's face as though made by a person's thumb, and a similar bruise on the left side, as if the woman's head had been pushed back and her throat then cut. There is a gash under the left ear reaching nearly to the center of the throat, and another cut apparently starting from the right ear. The neck is severed back to the vertebrae, which is also slightly injured. The abdominal wound are extraordinary for their length and the severity with which they have been inflicted. The deceased woman's clothes were loose, and the wounds could have been inflicted while she was dressed." The inquest will be held by Mr. Wynne E. Baxter, the coroner for the district, at the Working Lads' Institute, Whitechapel, at one o'clock today.

The investigation of Polly or Mary Ann Nichols's murder was not a major priority on the inspector's list. It seemed they were trying to write it off as an argument gone south or that it was done by a gang who bullies the women for money. They had so many different theories as to why this woman was murdered and left out in the open for everyone to see. It had only been a few days since I was starting to get an itch, almost like it had now become an addiction I soon needed a fix. I kept a low profile at work, only checking in when needed, when on duty, and even when I would do my time at the medical center, I kept to myself, but I would also make the necessary appearances at conferences to speak about the new techniques and procedures we were working on to advance the field forward. I stayed at the center a lot to have my presence known, to seem like I was working hard when all I was really doing was sitting in my quarters trying to figure out when I would attack again. I actually decided to go out for a stroll one evening to find my prey, to stalk them, learn their movements and make my move a few days later. I ended up meeting a lady of the night named Annie. I told her that I was just looking for companionship and that I wanted nothing more. She seemed hesitant and suspicious at first but after explaining I was a recently separated doctor who did not get out on the town much, she gave in and took a walk with me.
"What is your name then?"
"Oscar."
"Oscar, eh? Interesting name, never heard it before." I pushed aside the small annoyance growing inside of me, I needed to stay calm and collected. Keep it together until the right time. "What is your name?"
"Annie. Annie Chapman." Fitting.
"My mother's name was Annie."
"It is quite a common name for ladies these days, it seems like people just name their children after themselves. Selfish and narcissistic if you ask my piece on it." I did not. We walked in silence for a bit, "So, how is it that a doctor gets separated? I figure all the girls would be coming after you." I laughed, "Not all of them, not any of them. I fell in love and married my childhood sweetheart, she did not like or understand the demands of a doctor's career, especially those of a surgeon. She wanted me home more and I just could not give that to her."
"Ah, one of those working men. Nothing wrong with that."
"Not at all, and speaking of work, I should probably get back to it. Thank you for walking with me." I handed her the two bits we agreed upon to for the chat and I departed her company. She was perfect for what I needed.

It was the night of September eighth in which I decided to make my move These prostitutes are some of the most ignorant women, no, people I had ever encountered. They wandered in such areas that just welcomed an attack at any time. My patience was thin with them to begin with, the filthy whores. I was not

58

going to tolerate the stupidity, if they wanted to walk right into my arms, I would let them. I had one in my sights for the evening already, it would be easy to coax her to me. I checked in with the night nurse, so she could see that I had entered the building. I told her I would be in my quarters if I was needed, hoping I would not be called upon as there were other doctors available. I snuck out the window of my room, I decided to take my bag from work this time but only carry the supplies I would need, including a few containers. I walked the streets of Whitechapel, they were quite more lively this evening, it would be a good night to run into Annie because she would be out looking to make money. It did not take long to find her, she noticed and came to me right away, "'Ello Oscar, fine night for a walk, is it?" I nodded, looking around, hoping no one had heard her say my name. I would have to bide my time for this evening the streets had more people out and about, but seemed to be dying down. We headed in the direction that we normally do towards Hanbury Street, it may be my best shot because it would be quiet with everyone in that area being those who will need to be up early. "So, is it just the regular walk tonight or are you going to be requesting more? It costs more, just so you know." I nodded, "As it should, but I think it will just be a walk for the time being."

"Aye, sounds right to me then. How is your work going?" I shrugged, "As well as work for any surgeon can go, I suppose." She scoffed, "I never could be a surgeon, too many factors come along with it." We turned down Hanbury Street, Annie stopped a moment and turned to face me. "Are you sure you ain't wanting nothing more from me tonight?" She stepped in closer, leaning into me slightly. I felt repulsed and disgusted, these women were so tactless and disrespectful. I take into account that I was walking with a prostitute, a lady who makes her money by getting men to have their way with them, but this was just absurd. "Well, you have been so kind and patient with me, maybe it is time to try that. Will you?" She looked up at me, "Yes, of course." As she reached for my trousers, I grabbed the handkerchief I brought along with me, I grabbed her by the jaw "No..." was all she could get out before I stuff the handkerchief in her mouth, making it so she could not scream. I sliced her throat, wanting to hear that gurgling noise that had come along with Polly's death. It was like sweet music to my ears. She fell sideways into the fence, making a slight bang. I looked around to make sure no one had heard and come to investigate. All clear.

I went to work, I flipped the body over to see if I could cut in and break her neck internally, no such luck with my knife. Reminded myself to bring a better one for the job next time. Unsuccessful in the attempt to separate the neck, I flipped Annie back over. She was still struggling to breathe, "Just let go, there is no saving you, you will not survive. You are going to die." Annie's eyes widened at my words, she was still holding on to some kind of life, it was actually starting to frustrate and anger me. I wanted her to die quickly, or did I? Maybe suffering would be the route for her. To pay for what she had become, for the wretched, awful things she had done.

I know you think me a monster, I have been thought to be one since birth. Even before I began my new hobby. You can think me a monster all you want, but I am not. I am doing the world a service by getting rid of these disgusting creatures that call themselves women. They crawl upon the Earth, taking money for sexual favors and pleasure yet they can not seem to better themselves or take care of themselves. All drunken whores who just feed off of others. Just like Catherine, such a shame she got away from me. I would have had so much fun slicing her to bits.

Annie finally stopped trying to suck in air, her body went limp, her eyes lost all light of the here and now. She was gone. I could see my mother in this woman, short, plump, pallid, blue eyes shining out of her dark hair. I am sure she was a cold and heartless woman as well. I lifted her skirt, shuddering as I did. It made me feel dirty, unclean. I pulled out a surgical knife from the bag, made an incision in the upper abdomen, cutting her stomach open completely, pulling out the entirety of her intestines, cutting them completely from her body, leaving them on her shoulder. I removed her pelvis, her uterus, she would not be needing, she did not deserve, the upper portion of her vagina, and part of her bladder. I took these items and placed them in the jars I brought along with me, sticking them into my bag to take back. My souvenirs. Too bad I did not think to take any from Polly or the first Annie. There was light starting to show in the sky, I needed to hurry along. I packed everything up, wiping the instruments with the handkerchief to clean them, and I set my sail back to the Medical Center. I would need to grab some kind of sleep before my shift the next day. I climbed back in to my room as quietly as I could, making sure no one had seen me enter through the window. I put my things down and made my way to grab some water to take a quick bathe in. The night nurse was sitting at the station, "Well, you are up late, you are on morning duty are you not?" I nodded, "I just can not sleep this evening. My brain will not shut off. I was just coming out to grab some water to see if I can get some shut eye." She smiled slightly, "My George has horrible insomnia, he says he stays up throughout the entire night and can never figure out why. But, it is nice to have him go to bed with me when I get home in the mornings."
"Yes, I would imagine that would be a blessing."
"Oh, Doctor Melvin, I do apologize, that was very insensitive to your situation. I am so very sorry." I laughed, "Nurse Marchall, it is quite all right. I am not hung up on my wife leaving. It was something that was very much needed." I patted her hand, "I must try to get some kind of sleep in case I have anyone come in tomorrow." She furrowed her brow, "Sleep tight." I made my way back to my room, I take it that she did not mention anything about coming to need me that I was home free. I washed my face, washed my hands, pulled out my new found souvenirs in their respectable jars. I wondered if I would add them to the jars we had here so as not to call alarm when the examination of Annie's body is done that I have the exact body parts they will come to discover she is missing. I shrugged, stuffing them under the bed for the time being. I laid down on the bed, it seemed like it was more comfortable tonight than any other time before. I was literally beat. I closed my eyes and drifted into sleep.

Elizabeth stood before me, like so many times before. I was not unhappy that she began to visit my dreams again but they were so few and far between. This time she spoke to me, "Oscar, you should not do these things. These women do not deserve your anger and rage towards the people who hurt you in life. It is not worth getting caught and losing everything you have worked so hard for." She turned as if someone had called her name, I followed as she wandered through the alleyway, not sure of where we were exactly. She stopped outside of a gate, "You need to apologize to them." She pushed the gate open, I stepped around slowly, I was pulled into the yard by the corpses of the murdered women. I jumped awake, covered in sweat. Light flooded the room as I had forgotten to close the curtains when I returned the night before. I tried to wrap my brain around the contents of my dream, breathing heavily. That was not the kind of dreams I wanted to have, my dreams were the only way I could hold on to Elizabeth, to have her near and now she was handing me over to women I had killed. I was not going to let it change my mind. There was a knock on the door, making me jump slightly. I knew I would be on edge the entire day. I stood and pulled the door open, "Doctor Melvin, I am sorry to bother you, you did not do your normal morning check in and I was just making sure everything was all right." I nodded, "Yes, thank you Nurse. I am fine, just over slept a little. Had a very late night last night."
"You have an Inspector Abberline waiting for you in your office. He said it is quite urgent that he speak with the doctor on duty." My heart lept into my throat, he could not have known it was I who murdered Annie. I would assume they had found the body by now, it was light enough, someone would have stumbled upon her disgusting remains. "Um, just let him know I got a little held up with paperwork and I will be right in with him."
"Yes, Doctor." The nurse smiled and walked down the hall as I closed the door, rubbing my eyes to wake myself up. I did not want the detective to think I was incompetent. Not I.

"Sorry to keep you waiting, Detective. I got held up with some paperwork and just could not seem to catch up."
"Doctor Melvin, I presume?"
"Yes, Sir." He held his hand out, "I am Detective Inspector Frederick Abberline. I have been assigned to the murders that have happened recently." I sat down as not to look alarmed, "What can I do for you, Detective?"
"The body that was found this morning has led us to believe that the murderer is skilled or at least educated in the medical profession." I tried to look surprised, "What would lead you to that conclusion?"
"The murderer removed some of her body parts, cleanly, with precision. They had to know what they were doing. I am just canvassing the area, talking to all of the doctors, surgeons, medical professionals in the area to see where they may have been last night."
"I was here."
"Can you prove that?" I nodded, "Yes, I checked in with the night nurse and I was in my quarters all night. She can vouch that I did not leave, she would have seen me do so." The detective stared at me hard for a moment, his expression difficult

to read. I could only imagine what kind of fright I looked as I sat across from him, sleepless, sweaty, nerves on edge. "Well, then Doctor Melvin, that is really all I need from you right now then I suppose." I stood along with him, "Unless, you can answer this for me. Would you have any idea as to why a person would take organs from the woman they murdered?" I tried to sound shocked at this discovery, "He took her organs?" I twisted my face into a grimace, "I honestly would have no idea, unless the killer wanted it as a souvenir or if you say he is in the medical profession, something to examine or research? Many factors would be at play since we do not know who killed the woman. If they knew her, maybe it was for some reason linked to the relationship, if he did not, who knows?" Abberline nodded, "Yes, who knows? Well, good day, Sir. If I need to contact you further, I will be in touch."

"Yes, of course. Please, if there is anything I can do to help." He looked me up and down and made his way to the Nurse's station, I watched as he stopped to speak to the nurse on duty. I could not hear what they were saying, but he was no doubt, checking my alibi to see if I had been telling the truth. I waved as he turned towards me before making his way out the door. I felt like a fool. This was close, too close. I did not know what to do. Should I stop? No way, this was how I was going to change the world. Help get rid of the scum. I would be my own hero if no one else's. I needed to think of a plan, of a way to not link this back to me. I am sure that the detective would look past me as a suspect but I was not positive he would drop the medical professional idea. He was right, I had been too clean, too precise. I needed to be sloppier. Or did I? My nerves were on edge, I needed to find something to calm me down. I stepped back into my office and closed the door, I would send another letter to the police. I would make the game more interesting.

17th Sept 1888

Dear Boss

So now they say I am a Yid when will they lern Dear old Boss! You an me know the truth dont we. Lusk can look forever hell never find me but I am rite under his nose all the time. I watch them looking for me an it gives me fits ha ha I love my work an I shant stop until I get buckled and even then watch out for your old pal Jacky.

Catch me if you Can
Jack the Ripper

Sorry about the blood still messy from the last one. What a pretty necklace I gave her.

"Nurse, do you have anything for me?" She handed me two files, "You work too much, Doctor. You ever think about taking a vacation?" I leaned on the desk,

"Only if I can find a pretty little blonde to go along with me," I winked in fun, "Oh, Doctor Melvin, you are bad. You know my husband would not like that." "Who said I was talking about you?" I laughed light heartedly, "Oh, would you be so kind as to send this out in the mail today?" I winked at her and made my way to the examination rooms. A young woman sat in the first one, "Hello, Miss..." my heart sank as I opened the folder with the young patient's file in it, "Miss Melvin."

Chapter Twelve

The young woman looked up, she did not seem to recognize me. As much as I would have liked it to be my Elizabeth, it was not. "It is a coincidence. My name is Doctor Melvin. Oscar Melvin." She smiled slightly, the name not phasing her, I thought maybe she could have been somehow related or maybe even someone crazy enough to marry one of my brothers. "I see that you are suffering from severe headaches?" She nodded, "Yes, I have had horrible headaches. I can not eat, I can not sleep, it's interfering with my work. I thought it was just the weather change but they just keep getting worse."

"I see." I stood up, washing my hands. "I am going to feel around, just to see where the pain is originating from." I put my hands on her head, it would have been so easy to just snap her neck. I shook my head of the thought, she was a nice girl. A respectable girl. "So, what do you do for work, Miss Melvin?"

"I work the desk at a bank nearby."

"I see, so headaches can definitely interfere with work. Let me know where the pain is the worst." She took my hand, moving it to the left side of the back of her head. Right above the crook in the neck. "Do you sit a lot or lift heavy items?" She nodded, "I sometimes help move the bags of money in the safe, I handle deliveries and such as well." I nodded, "Let me see if I can help you out here without having to go further, lie down on your stomach, I think your issue may be in your neck and shoulder area." I ran my hand along the base of her neck, right above the shoulder line. I pushed in slightly under her neck, feeling a slight pop, "Oh, that felt wonderful." I pushed down again on the other side, another pop. "This is most likely where your problem stems from, when you sit at the desk, your shoulders get slumped or slouched and they just get into a little niche and you just have to have them adjusted back out." She sat up, rubbing her neck, moving it around in circles. "Thank you, Doctor. It feels slightly better already." I smiled, "Just try to sit with your shoulders back and try not to lift too much. I know it is part of your job but it could really do some damage. We do not want long term problems." She stood, grabbing her coat and purse. "Miss Melvin, forgive me if this is too forward a question, are you married?" She blushed, "No. Why do you ask?"

"Well, I do not want to be rude or give the wrong impression, but when I was younger, I was separated from my family. I have not seen them in many years and when you came in with the last name Melvin, you would be very close to the ages of my brothers. I thought maybe there was some relation." She smiled slightly, "I am terribly sorry to hear that, I really wish I could have helped. I am not married, I was however adopted by a family that had two boys. They never mentioned having a sibling that was lost though." I shrugged, "Were their names Peter and James?"

"No, they are Michael and Paul."

"Well, the surname Melvin is common here I guess."

"I am sorry I could not be of help. I really wish I could have been. Thank you so much for helping with my headaches, Doctor. I hope you find your family." I nodded, "Thank you, see the nurse on the way out and she will get you discharge papers." She nodded, closing the door behind her as she left. I felt angry and sad all at the same time, like life was dangling the chance to find Elizabeth and then pulled it right out from under me. I needed something to take my mind off of it. On to my next patient.

It was a quiet day at the center, which was good in a way. Not a lot of injured people, but of course it makes for a boring day and smaller pay at the end of the day. I sat in my office most of the day, thinking of the past few weeks. I had a total of three murders on my hands, even if the detectives say I was not the cause of Annie Millwood's death, I will take the credit.

A few weeks had passed, the investigation on the murders was still running pretty high. I had taken a break on the murders, I just loved the fact that everyone was so scared, no one knew when the murderer would strike again, when he would come out to play. They were looking at so many different people as suspects. People from the medical field, the show district, and even royalty. How they came to that conclusion is beyond me. I decided to have a little fun with them, I sent in a letter. It read as follows:

Dear Boss,

I keep on hearing the police have caught me but they wont fix me just yet. I have laughed when they look so clever and talk about being on the right track. That joke about Leather Apron gave me real fits. I am down on whores and I shant quit ripping them till I do get buckled. Grand work the last job was. I gave the lady no time to squeal. How can they catch me now. I love my work and want to start again. You will soon hear of me with my funny little games. I saved some of the proper red stuff in a ginger beer bottle over the last job to write with but it went thick like glue and I cant use it. Red ink is fit enough I hope ha. ha. The next job I do I shall clip the ladys ears off and send to the police officers just for jolly wouldn't you. Keep this letter back till I do a bit more work, then give it out straight. My knife's so nice and sharp I want to get to work right away if I get a chance. Good Luck.

Yours truly
Jack the Ripper

Dont mind me giving the trade name

PS Wasnt good enough to post this before I got all the red ink off my hands curse it No luck yet. They say I'm a doctor now. ha ha

I decided to pick a name for myself, one that would get their attention, strike even more fear into their miserable little hearts. No one had to worry except for those worthless whores. I made the plans to make a trip out within the next few days, grab me another one. Make it a good one this time, really go to town on her. Show them, I do not plan to stop anytime soon. I was interrupted in my thoughts when a knock came to the door. I was almost annoyed with my work, so many needy people. I pulled the door open, visibly frustrated. I knew I should not have been as I chose this role in life, I chose the role to save lives, even though I had come to enjoy taking them more. "Doctor Melvin, Inspector Abberline is here to speak with you." I nodded, "Thank you, I will be out in just a moment." She nodded with a slight smile, "Are you feeling okay? You look a little pale." "I am fine. Just tired."

I stepped into the office, "Inspector, what do I owe this visit?" "I think you know, Doctor Melvin." I stopped in my tracks, "Am I supposed to?" Abberline cleared his throat, "I know you are a highly intelligent man." "I like to think so, is there something I have missed?" My heart was pounding, pulse racing. Had Abberline somehow linked one or all of these women back to me? Had I messed up in some way? Had someone seen me? Was he here to arrest me?

"The last time I was here, you said that you were in your room all night. The nurse at the front also attested to this statement yet one of the other doctors said that he knocked on your door around two a.m that morning and you did not answer. Can you explain why this may have been?" My heart felt as if it was going to explode. No, I could not explain this, why had no one told me that someone had come looking for me that night? "I may have been sleeping hard and not heard the knock."

"Do you find that to be a little on the dangerous side, Doctor? What if there were an emergency, like there was that very evening." "If there was a serious emergency, they would have entered the room to wake me that way." I kept eye contact with the Inspector as not to look as if I was hiding anything. "And, as you pointed out, the nurse attested that I had not left the building and there is always at least one at the desk all night. Someone definitely would have seen me leave if I had done so. Are you accusing me of murder?" Abberline just stared at me, "No, Sir. I was just getting a follow up on your statement as we do when stories do not align. That is all that I need. Thank you for your time." I stood up, "No need to see me out, Doctor. I know the way. Have a good day." By the end of the conversation, I was almost terrified that I had been caught but I was also angry that the detective tried to question my intelligence. I had thought about putting off going out and finding more whores to kill, but this put me over the edge. Tonight, I would leave the center, tell the nurses I was heading home. I would not have an alibi if the Inspector came poking around after these murders but when you live alone, how can you have an alibi? I gave no reason to be put under a microscope, only because I was a surgeon? There were many others in the medical field, many other theories they had about this killer. I do not know why I was so mad. I actually was the killer, I was the man taking lives. His visit had nothing to do with that though and this is where my rage stemmed from.

"Well, Victoria, I think I will actually be heading home this evening. Think it might be a good night to sleep in my own bed for once."
"You do work too much, Doctor Melvin. It will be good for you to take a full night off, get some rest." I signed my name on the Check Out line and made my way home, this way my neighbors would also see me going inside. Once they were all asleep, I would make my way back out. I had all the time in the world.

I made my way back out around eleven that night. I was going to see what I could find roaming the streets and if I found nothing, so be it. Of course, luck would have it about an hour or so later, I ran into another old bat wandering around drunk out of her skull. This one was not much shorter than I, she was pale as if she was already halfway to her deathbed. Curly hair, light eyes, plump. They all are, why are they all so disgusting? How horrid are the men who have to pay them for their services? Gross. "Good evening," I said as I walked by her, "Evenin' to you too." She had a thick accent, sideways is what I called it. Cockney I believe is what others refer to it as. "Nice night for a stroll don't you think?"
"If'n you like strolls, I guess." She walked beside me, "Do you like strolls?" She shrugged, "Eh, now and den. Sure." She took my arm, "So, whatcha fancy?"
"Just a stroll for now." I continued on without looking at her, she disgusted me. She smelled and just felt dirty.
We walked until I could not contain myself anymore, I pulled her into Dutfield's Yard, leaned against the fence, "So, what do you offer then?" She shook her head, "No, not tonight. Some other night then." I was not going to let her waste my time, I grabbed a hold of her, she let out a scream. I could not take the chance of someone seeing me, I slashed her throat and ran. I heard voice call out behind me. Shit. Seeing a man round the corner. I was not going to be caught now, not after I had gotten away with, not because this whore screamed out, I took off down the alley way. He followed. I had no idea where to run, I was not familiar with this area. I turned down a side street, he kept pace with me pretty good. I could not let him get a good look at me, I pulled my hat down as far as I could and pushed myself to run as fast as my legs would carry me. The railroad tracks were ahead of me, I was not sure which way to turn. Not sure which way to go, I ducked down an alley way, with just enough time to duck behind a dumpster before the man caught up to me. He looked around but kept going. I waited for a few moments more before coming out from my hiding place, just to make sure the coast was clear.

I found it odd that the man followed me for so long, even with the chance to catch the dreaded Ripper, you would think they would have given up on me and went back to check on the whore. She was done for. I decided to take a walk, clear my head, get some much needed fresh air. To my surprise, I ran straight into another whore. Dare I take two in one night? I dared. "Well, Miss, what are you doing out so late a psychotic murderer on the loose?"

"I ain't afraid of no loose murderer. Some man running around with a knife, it's happened before." She shot back, "Oh, are you not? I would be, especially if I was a lady of the night. Especially if I were you."

"What's that supposed to mean?" I grabbed her, covering her mouth so she could not scream, this one was not ruining the fun for me. I slashed her throat right away, her eyes went wide as she stared at me while falling to the ground, trying to crawl away from me as she struggled for breath, struggled for life. I went up behind her, striking her in the back of the head, just enough to stop her. I rolled her over onto her back, I was not waiting for her to die to get my work done. I sliced her from the breast to the pelvis, ripped her intestines out, throwing them up to her shoulder, cutting a good piece and put it between her arm and her body. Her attempt to scream came out as just a sigh of wind, almost a whistle. Not quite. I slashed at her again, nicking her ear just right, a piece fell off onto the ground, I ripped a part of her clothing, wrapping the ear like a present. They would get a kick out of that, at least I would. She tried to fight back, waving her arms at me, she was a tough broad. I slashed at her face, cutting into her eyelid and scratching her nose, hitting other parts of her face in a wild thrashing of rage. I did not like that she was fighting me, I was stronger than her, she should be dying. I pulled her skin from her breast to her vaginal bone open, like her insides were on display for all to see. The bubble of rage inside me rising. I stabbed her in the liver multiple times, jaggedly gashing it in various places. I decided to leave her navel in tact, but made cuts around it to look like it was smiling, a little jab to the groin, a gash in the pancreas, slices here, slashes there. I took my time but hurried to get away from the scene. I finished up once I worked out all of my anger, put my instruments away, I headed towards the police station. I needed to leave another little note for Detective Inspector Abberline.

I headed home right after, needed to get my instruments and myself cleaned up. I had a feeling once the Detective was called upon, I would be as well. I was not wrong, not long after two thirty, there was a knock on my door. I was surprised he would be calling on me at home. I mussed my hair and made myself look as sheepishly as I could. Opening the door, I acted surprised, "Inspector, what an interesting surprise."

"Get dressed, there has been another murder, I need you to come with me." I put my best confused look on, "You want me to inspect the body?"

"I want you to come and watch the other doctor examine the body, I need a second pair of eyes. Intelligent, young eyes to make sure nothing is missed." I nodded, "Let me get dressed." I, of course, grabbed clothes that I had not worn recently, just in case anyone reported what the killer had been wearing. "Do you always wear hat?" I nodded, "Yes, I was born with a deformity that I do not enjoy being poked at about, so I wear the hat so no one can see it." He nodded, "I see." We arrived at the scene, a large crowd had formed. "Do this many people usually come out to watch?"

"The people enjoy the gore, they want to know as much as they can so they know how to avoid getting the slice themselves." I nodded, "I see." I enjoyed making the scene, but as a doctor, I had respect for privacy. Mongrels. "Doctor Frederick

Brown, this is Doctor Melvin. He is going to be following you around, I want a second pair of eyes on this. In case anything is missed." Doctor Brown did not look amused, he seem agitated that I was even there. I shrugged it off, old doctors always get set in their ways and offended when their judgment is called into play. "Okay, are you ready, I am going to talk as I examine the body. Get those notebooks handy Gentlemen." I stifled a laugh, was this guy serious?
"The body is on its back, the head turned to left shoulder. The arms by the side of the body as if they had fallen there. Both palms upwards, the fingers slightly bent. The left leg extended in a line with the body. The abdomen is exposed. Right leg bent at the thigh and knee. The throat cut across. The intestines were drawn out to a large extent and placed over the right shoulder -- they were smeared over with some feculent matter. We have seen this before in another murder, so I am guessing this is the same killer. A piece of about two feet was quite detached from the body and placed between the body and the left arm, apparently by design. The lobe and auricle of the right ear were cut obliquely through. There is a quantity of clotted blood on the pavement on the left side of the neck round the shoulder and upper part of arm, and fluid blood-coloured serum which had flowed under the neck to the right shoulder, the pavement sloping in that direction. Body is quite warm. No death stiffening has taken place. She must have been dead most likely within the half hour. No blood on the skin of the abdomen or secretion of any kind on the thighs. No spurting of blood on the bricks or pavement around. No marks of blood below the middle of the body. There was no blood on the front of the clothes. There were no traces of recent connexion." I followed the doctor around the scene, almost mockingly, I took a look at the body, trying to make it as if this was the first time I had seen it. "There seems to be extensive internal damage, some body parts have been removed and others are severely damaged." Doctor Brown seemed less than amused by my cutting in, he continued with his briefing, "I would say that death was immediate." Wrong on that one, Buddy. This old broad put up a good fight, she still lost the battle in the end, but a good fight none the less. "I will have more for you once I can get the body back to the morgue to have it looked over." Abberline nodded, "Take Melvin with you." Doctor Brown sighed, "I prefer to work alone if that is all right, too many hands on deck could possibly contaminate the examination." Abberline turned towards him, "I believe I said take Melvin with you." The doctor nodded, "Yes Inspector," he turned to me and motioned for me to follow him. An officer brought Abberline a piece of paper, after reading it, he crumpled it between his hands and sighed, pretty sure it was my letter I left for him. I am rather glad I got to enjoy his moment.

We arrived with the body arrived at Golden Lane, some of the blood was dispersed through the removal of the body to the mortuary. I helped Brown remove the clothes from the deceased woman's body, I was highly amused when a piece of her ear dropped from the clothing, into his hand. There was a green discoloration over the abdomen. After washing the left hand carefully, a bruise the size of a sixpence, recent and red, was discovered. I had really done a number on her face as it was very much mutilated. There was a cut about a quarter of an inch through the lower left eyelid, dividing the structures completely through. The upper eyelid on that side, there was a scratch through the skin on the left upper eyelid, near to the angle of the nose. The right eyelid was cut through to about half an inch. There was a deep cut over the bridge of the nose, extending from the left border of the nasal bone down near the angle of the jaw on the right side of the cheek. The cut extended an inch and a half, parallel with the lower lip. There was on each side of cheek a cut which peeled up the skin, forming a triangular flap about an inch and a half. On the left cheek there were two abrasions of the epithelium under the left ear.

"The throat was cut across to the extent of about six or seven inches. The large vessels on the left side of the neck were severed. The larynx was severed below the vocal chord. All these injuries were performed by a sharp instrument like a knife, and pointed." Brown said, as if that was not an obvious observation.

We examined the abdomen. The front walls were laid open from the breast bones to the pubes. The cut commenced opposite the enciform cartilage. The incision went upwards, not penetrating the skin that was over the sternum.
Behind this, the liver was stabbed as if by the point of a sharp instrument. Below this was another incision into the liver of about two and a half inches, and below this the left lobe of the liver was slit through by a vertical cut. Two cuts were shewn by a jagging of the skin on the left side. The abdominal walls were divided in the middle line to within a quarter of an inch of the navel. The cut then took a horizontal course for two inches and a half towards the right side. It then divided round the navel on the left side, and made a parallel incision to the former horizontal incision, leaving the navel on a tongue of skin. Attached to the navel was two and a half inches of the lower part of the rectus muscle on the left side of the abdomen. The incision then took an oblique direction to the right and was shelving. The incision went down the right side of the vagina and rectum for half an inch behind the rectum.

"There was a stab of about an inch on the left groin. This was done by a pointed instrument. I draw the conclusion that the act was made after death, and there would not have been much blood on the murderer. The cut was made by someone on the right side of the body, kneeling below the middle of the body. The intestines had been detached to a large extent from the mesentery. About two feet of the colon was cut away and was most likely what we found lying in between the body and the arm. There was a cut from the upper part of the slit on the under surface of the liver to the left side, and another cut at right angles to this, which were about an inch and a half deep and two and a half inches long. Liver itself was healthy. The pancreas was cut, but not through, on the left side of the spinal column. The left renal artery was cut through. I would say that someone who knew the position of the kidney must have done it. The lining membrane over the uterus was cut through. The womb was cut through horizontally, leaving a stump of three quarters of an inch. The rest of the womb had been taken away with some of the ligaments. The vagina and cervix of the womb was uninjured. I believe the wound in the throat was first inflicted. I believe she must have been lying on the ground. I believe the perpetrator of the act must have had considerable knowledge of the position of the organs in the abdominal cavity and the way of removing them. It required a great deal of medical knowledge to have removed the kidney and to know where it was placed. The parts removed would be of no use for any professional purpose. I think the perpetrator of this act had sufficient time, or he would not have nicked the lower eyelids. It would take at least five minutes. I cannot assign any reason for the parts being taken away. I feel sure that there was no struggle, and believe it was the act of one person. The throat had been so instantly severed that no noise could have been emitted. I should not expect much blood to have been found on the person who had inflicted these wounds. The wounds could not have been self-inflicted." Abberline nodded at the testament of Doctor Brown, "Melvin, do you have anything to add?" I shook my head, "No Sir, we both went over the body quite extensively. I agree that his words pretty much sum up the wounds, although, I am not quite sure the victim was lying down when the throat was slashed. There is an odd layout to the trail it left. May I?" Brown looked furious with me, I took him by the arm and face him towards me, "Now, you are taller than the victim, but we are not sure of the height of the killer, so I would assume the killer thrust the knife like so and went this way. I feel the victim was standing and went downwards as the throat was cut." I demonstrated a couple ways as not to give the exact way it happened, I did not want to look as if I had too much knowledge and become a suspect once again. Abberline nodded, "Well, thank you for your input. I must get back to the station, I am sure the papers will have a field day with this one. This is the worst yet. This is pure rage and anger showing through."

The next morning, I made sure to check out the paper as soon as I arrived to work. I knew that Abberline would hand over the letter I had left for him. He would not leave such a piece of evidence out. I felt a bit saucy, so I left it on a postcard. Just as I suspected, the paper had it published.

I was not codding dear old Boss when I gave you the tip, you'll hear about Saucy Jacky's work tomorrow double event this time number one squealed a bit couldn't finish straight off. ha not the time to get ears for police. thanks for keeping last letter back till I got to work again.

Jack the Ripper

Double event. I could only imagine how Abberline felt, I knew I was feeling pretty damn high and mighty.

Chapter Thirteen

Sitting at my desk the next day, thinking about how I got away with two murders in one night, within two hours of each other. I could not believe it, I really could not. I heard a commotion start up outside, voices yelling all at once. I made my way out to see what could have been going on. "What do you intend to do about the murders, Inspector?" One man yelled from a large crowd, "It has been going on for months now and you have not made any arrests!" Yelled another. "We do not feel safe in the streets anymore."

"Five women have been killed, why do you not have more police in the streets? Especially late at night." Inspector Abberline raised his hands as if to quiet everyone, "Look, Ladies and Gentlemen, I understand your plight, I really do. The reason we have not added more officers to the streets is we do not have the man power to do so. We have been doing all that we can to find this killer. He is a very intelligent professional, he knows a lot about what he is doing and he leaves no trace behind. We have a description as there was a witness who followed him just last night. We also have the new Scotland Yard being built and it will be finished quite soon. While, I can not guarantee when we will make an arrest, I can guarantee that we will. I promise that we will not stop looking until we find this monster." That word made my head spin, my heart skip, and my veins turn to ice. I loathed that words. I walked over to the mob that surrounded Abberline, catching his eyes. I stood silent in the back of the crowd, I stared stone cold at him, trying to send the message that this would continue and he would not find the killer. I was now pushed to my limits. You may think me a monster but I was made into this. I was forced to this. I was pushed to this.

I had thought about taking a break from murdering another whore because there was such a close call last night but Abberline's speech sparked more rage in me. I would not let him or anyone else scare me into backing down. I was not sure when my next attack would be but I would be out every night scoping the streets, setting up for my next kill. I noticed Abberline making his way over to me, pushing his way through the crowd who was still shouting questions at him. "Doctor Melvin, good afternoon. May I have a word with you?" I nodded, "Sure, would you like to step into the center?" Abberline shook his head, "No, it is not anything that will take much time."

"It never is," I smiled. "It is just, when I asked you to overlook the crime scene with Doctor Brown, I was hoping that you could shed some light on something that maybe he had overlooked. I know this was our most extensive murder yet, I just wanted a fresh pair of eyes to maybe catch something that Doctor Brown may have missed."

"Well, Inspector, Doctor Brown covered everything. I went over the crime scene and the body with him and I did not find anything beyond what he had."

Abberline nodded, "It is just we have really hit a wall with this and I worry that we may not be able to catch this killer," he cleared his throat, "that stays between us." I nodded, "We will call it doctor patient confidentiality."

"I really hope this new facility can give us more room, more eyes on the streets, more procedures. I have hit my wits end with it, I really have."

"Well, God forbid the killer strike again, but if he does, you are more than welcome to call on myself for a second pair of eyes. I do not know what I can offer beyond Doctor Brown or Doctor Odersand, but I can try my best."

Abberline stuck his hand out, I shook it. "Thank you, Doctor. It is comforting to know there are still good men in this world." Good men. I was a good man.

I turned the lamp off in my office, sat in the dark for a few moments before making my way to the doctor's quarters. I decided to stay in that particular evening, I was tired and wanted to rest up before I began stalking my next prey. I lit a candle, setting it on the bedside table. I recounted my conversation with Abberline from earlier that afternoon. I almost began to question if he was toying with me, maybe I could come up with something on this next murder to throw him off my trail. They had linked four murders to the same killer, but there were others, other ones that were not even looked at twice. Other murders that they kept to themselves because they did not have the same details as those that I had performed. I was not the only killer on the loose and I would use that to my favor. I decided to start keeping a log and a journal of my days, of my thoughts, maybe sometime in the future, when I had passed on, they would find it, they would realize how stupid they were. They would find out it was me the whole time. I undressed myself, laying my clothes on the chair in the corner. Sitting on the bed, I ran my hands through my hair, feeling the lump on my head, it had been a while since I had let anyone see it. It had been a while since I had let anyone laugh at and tease me for it. I kept it hidden all the time, I was long past my Circus days where I walked around openly. As much as I despised that horrid place, as much as I was beaten and hated by Colton, I was accepted by more than I had ever been accepted before. I actually almost missed the place, I thought about reaching out to Iris and Thomas to check in on how things were going. I stretched out on the bed, feeling slightly lost, slightly out of place. I know I picked this career, this life, this path, I just could not make sense of it anymore. After Catherine left me, I felt as if I had lost my way. I stopped trying to further my career to my own practice and became content with my work at the Medical Center. It was not where I would stay forever, of course, but I felt a lack of passion in saving lives and took on a passion for taking them. I had become the monster that everyone had deemed me. I was not sorry, I would never be sorry. I was not remorseful, they brought this on themselves. Every single one of them. I would make a joke of the police, I would make a spectacle of the whores, and I would make history. They would never catch me.

They never did.

I forced myself to stop thinking and to get some sleep. I hoped that the next day would come and go soon, tomorrow I would strike again. Tomorrow I would leave a corpse that would throw them off of the trail they have been going down. I drifted to sleep, I was pleasantly surprised that Elizabeth visited me.

She reached out for my hand, smiling at me. I was overjoyed when our hands connected and I made the realization that I could touch her now. I could feel her. She was still a little girl in my dreams, not much older than I was when I was kid napped. I was slightly worried and not sure whether or not this meant that she was still a part of this Earth. I had never been able to touch her before in my dreams. I had never been able to feel her warmth, I only recently was able to communicate with her, "Ozzie, you have to come with me. Let me show you." She pulled me along behind her. I wondered how she saw me, was I still a child to her as well or did she see me as the man I was. I let her pull me along the hallway, I was not sure where we were. I did not care, I was with my Elizabeth and all was well in the world. We stopped in an alley way, Elizabeth pulling me next to her. We were looking up at the new Scotland Yard, I recognized the building even if it was dark and out of focus to me. I heard a sound, almost like a girl crying. I looked around, had Elizabeth actually showed me to my next victim? Was she helping me in some way through my dreams? I did not understand, "Lizzie, what does this mean?"
"She will be left here, Ozzie. This is where you will leave her, part of her. This is where you will send your message." She smiled, turned from me, and disappeared. I opened my eyes, it was still dark in the room. I did not jump awake nor was I sweating from my dreams like I had always done in the past. I sat up calmly. I knew what Elizabeth was telling me, she was right. I needed to send a message, I needed to get the police off of my trail. I decided to go back to sleep, rolling over, closing my eyes. Elizabeth did not return to me, nothing did. I slept a dreamless sleep.

I was not scheduled the next day so I was in no hurry to roll out of bed when I awoke to the sun peeking in the room. I laid in bed for another hour before getting up to go out and wander the streets. I needed to scope out the new Scotland Yard building, I needed to know how I could get into the basement where I was planning to leave the body of my latest victim. I knew I would take a different route with this murder, I would choose a young girl this time to get away from the older women I had been leaving behind. Completely turn the tables on the whole investigation. I stopped into a lovely tea shop where the head maid was a young, beautiful woman. I would have guessed her age around twenty-five. She was full of life, full of brightness. Her eyes lit up the room and almost blinded me when she smiled, "Welcome, can I get you some tea, Sir?" I nodded, "Yes, I would love a cup of tea and do you have any pastries?" She nodded, "We have some of the best pies in London." She said with a slight wink. I took a seat at a table nearby the window, "Are you local?"
"I am. I work at the medical center."

"A doctor huh? Well, welcome to my tea shop, just give me a shout if you need anything else, name is Molly." She smiled and was off to the next customer. I almost loathed her at the same time I almost loved her. She radiated such an energy, too bad I would be taking that from her. She would be my next target, she would be my message.

I finished my tea and had a few cheese danish, I was now off to get my plan going into motion.

I watched and waited, Molly was finishing up closing for the evening. She did not have anyone around to walk her home, to keep her safe. She locked up and started in the direction that I imagined would be her way home. I followed behind her a distance as to not draw attention to myself and to not alarm her. The last thing I needed right then was another woman to scream. I was even less familiar with this area than the one I barely escaped before. She turned down a dark alley, this was my moment. I walked up behind her, as quietly as I could, grabbing her by the throat, covering her mouth. I sliced. Deep. I let her fall to the ground, body convulsing. I opened my bag, pulled out my bone saw I had brought along. This was going to be a special treat, I had been planning it all day. Once her body gave up, all life drained, I went to work. I cut into her vertebrae, removing her head completely then I cut her arms and legs off. Just the torso would be left for the amazing Detective Inspector Abberline. I would leave it in the new Scotland Yard, forever tainting the building. Forever letting it be known that they had a murder on their own home turf. I pulled out a garbage bag I had shoved in my medical bag, I put the pieces of her body into it. I threw the arms, legs, and head into the Thames. Walking back to the Scotland Yard building, looking around to make sure the coast was clear, I laid the torso of the body down, pulling her dress down to expose her breasts. I wanted this to be as gruesome a scene as possible. I wanted her to be on display, I wanted her to be vulnerable even beyond death. I quickly packed up and headed home, I am sure there would be someone to do their lookout rounds coming through soon. I returned home right before two a.m, good thing I did not live far from the area. I wondered how long it would take to find Molly's body, if they would come to fetch me to help give my professional opinion. I was not sure how I would react. Surprised or not that this murder had happened, it would definitely throw them off the scent and make them think there was more than one killer, that is if my plan worked. I cleaned myself up, hid my medical bag, and disposed of the bloody towels.

My plan worked almost like clockwork, a knock to my door around four in the morning pulled me from my thoughts and my writing. I made myself look disheveled as if I had been taking advantage of my night off and getting some shut eye. No other than Detective Inspector Frederick Abberline stood in my doorway, a grim look on his face. "Doctor Melvin,"

"Another murder I assume?" He nodded, "Let me grab my bag." I did not even bother to get properly dressed, I put my coat on over my medical clothes. Off we went.

There she was, Molly, in all of her glory. I was proud of myself for the display I put her in. All of the men were looking at her, they could not look away, she was exposed to the highest regard. I could not have been more accomplished in my goal I set out to do. "Can you believe this?" I overheard one officer say, "Right here in our new headquarters. Someone is very brave."

"Maybe a little too brave, more so in the cocky category if you ask me. Too big for his britches."

Abberline stopped and looked at me, "This is a mockery of the department. I need to find this man, I need to bring him down. We are the laughing stock of the city."

"With all due respect, Detective Abberline, the city does not understand the inner workings of an investigation. I mean, I hardly understand it myself as to how this man does what he does and has not been caught. Did I hear you had a description of him did you not?"

"Aye, we do, but nothing that makes him stand out from the hundreds of other gentlemen in the same height and age range." I nodded, "Well, let me take a look at her, I will see what I can see."

"Thank you, they also called in another doctor as well, get as many perspectives as we possibly can."

We did our inspection, nothing but the rotting torso of a young woman. The final report read as follows:

Doctor Thomas Bond took the lead as I tried to keep a lower profile as not to have my hand in every investigation until Abberline trusted me enough to be given the lead and final word.

"On October second, shortly before four in the morning, I was called to the new police buildings along with another local surgeon, Doctor Oscar Melvin. We were brought in and there shown the decomposed trunk of a woman. It was then lying in the basement and partially unwrapped. I visited the vault where it was found, and saw that the wall against which it had lain was stained black. The sixth cervical vertebra had been sawn through in removing the head from the trunk. The lower limbs and pelvis had been removed, and the four lumbar vertebrae had been sawn through by a series of long, sweeping cuts. The skin of the torso was clear of any wounds. The skin was light. Both arms had been removed at the shoulder joints by several incisions. The cuts had apparently been made obliquely from above downwards, and then round the arms. The neck had been divided by several jagged incisions at the bottom of the larynx, which had been sawn through. The rib cartilages were not ossified. In connection with the heart there were indications that convinced me that the woman did not die of suffocation or drowning. The liver was normal, and the stomach contained about an ounce of partly digested food. Portions of the body were missing. Going by the length of the torso, the condition of the skin and the state of bones, the victim was around twenty - four or twenty - five years of age. It appeared that she was full fleshed, well nourished, with a fair skin and dark hair. The appearances went to prove that deceased had never borne, or at any rate had never suckled a child. The body had not been in the water."

"Thank you, Gentlemen. You have been a great help, especially at such a horrid hour to pull you from your time off. I appreciate the hard work that you have put forth to help the department." Detective Abberline seemed to be stumped with this murder. He pulled me aside, "Between you and I, I can not say this was done by the same man who murdered the other women. This one is different in so many ways, I am not sure if I should add her to Ripper deaths. Then again, he could be trying to throw us off or maybe this is a new pattern he wants to begin." I shrugged, "I am truly at a loss for words on this, Detective."
I stood inside the police station, wondering why Abberline had called me back. We had just left each other earlier that morning after I helped with the Whitehall Mystery Woman who was no mystery to me. "Doctor Melvin, I am terribly sorry to pull you from the center, I know you have been quite busy, but we have found something that I think will be of interest." I followed him down the long hallway, down the stairs, into the bottom part of the police station where they sometimes kept the bodies of ongoing murder investigations, it smelled horribly. He led me to a room where the body was laid out on a gurney, an arm laid on the table next to it. "We found this arm in the River Thames just about an hour ago, right before I sent my man to call on you. I think it belongs to our Jane Doe." I perked an eyebrow up, "Well, if it does not, there is someone else missing limbs out there." I put on a pair of gloves and picked up the arm, I examined it closely as if it was the first time I had ever seen it before. I walked around and lined the arm up with the shoulder of the corpse. I looked at Abberline and nodded, "I think it most definitely is hers."
"Would you be willing to make a statement?" I shrugged, "Why not?"

About an hour or so later, Abberline had called a group of random newsmen to the station, he had me set up out front with my statement ready to go.
"About two hours ago, detectives discovered an arm in the River Thames after doing a sweep of the area for possible clues after finding a headless, limbless torso in the buildings of the new Scotland Yard. I closely examined an arm that was brought to the mortuary, and I found that it accurately fitted the trunk. The hand was long and appeared to be very well shaped. Apparently it was the hand of a person not used to manual labor, so we are not looking for any missing factory women. All the cuts on the trunk seemed to have been made after death. There was nothing to indicate the cause of death, though as the inside of the heart was pale and free from clots, it probably arose from haemorrhage or fainting. From a series of measurements we took we came to the conclusion that the woman was about five foot, eight inches in height".

The men started asking questions, "Do we think this murder is in connection with the ones we have seen in the recent months?"
"I honestly can not answer that, due to the circumstances and the differences in this crime scene as opposed to the ones in the past, it is likely this may be a new

killer who is trying to either push the crime off on the original killer or it could definitely be the same killer just trying to throw us for a loop."

"Are there any leads as to whom this may be? Have there been any arrests made in connection with these murders?"

I looked to Detective Abberline to field this question, he stepped forward, "There have been a few brought in for questioning, we have been looking into a few suspects, though they have all had solid alibis. This killer is very intelligent, he leaves nothing to trace behind. We do have a description as a young man came upon him while he was in the midst of a murder and chased him. The only problem we have run into is it is a very vague description and it could be just about anyone."

"What is the description, Detective Abberline?" He cleared his throat, "Well, the man said the killer is around five foot, seven inches. Medium build, in his late twenties to early thirties with a trim, clean cut mustache. Very common these days, but we are trying all we can to apprehend and bring him down. That is all we have for now." He led me back into the station where he had me sit and relax until the media crowd died down outside. He did not want me bogged down with questions that I did not have the answers to. "Would you like some tea, Doctor?" I nodded, "Sounds good."

"You know, I must say, at first I really thought you could have been the Ripper. Such a secretive, mysterious man. I surely thought we had you when the other surgeon had his story not match up with yours. I was ready to arrest you." I took a sip of tea, "Why did you not, if I may ask." He sat down in a chair opposite the desk from me, "Not sure to be honest. I am honestly not sure I believe you are an innocent man. Then again, I do not know who is innocent and who is not these days. But, I did not arrest you because I felt you would come in handy, and if you are not in fact the killer, I need you out there to help." I nodded, "Well, I will help as much as I can, I do not have any more knowledge than the next guy, but I can give you my insight when you need."

"I am grateful for that."

"I should be heading back to the center, work calls." Abberline stood up with me, I nodded, "Take a rest, Detective. I shall see myself out." We shook hands and I was on my way.

When I returned to the medical center, the nurse smiled, "You have a visitor waiting for you in your office." I nodded, "Oh, do you know who it is?" She nodded, "Your wife, Catherine." My blood immediately began to boil. She was the last person I wanted to see right now or ever. "Thank you, Nurse." She nodded and went back to her paperwork. I took my time getting to my office, wondering what Catherine could have wanted. Why she had come to see me. I pushed the door open, "Hi Ozzie." She was definitely showing in her stages of pregnancy. "I vividly remember telling you not to call me that." She looked at the floor, "What do you want, Catherine?"

"I have been thinking, I do not think this baby is the other man's and I want to come home. I want to work on us. I can get around you staying at work late." She looked at me, "You have the nerve to come here and tell me that this baby is

mine? I know it is not. Do not try to play me for a fool, I am an intelligent man."
My voice began to rise, I tried to keep calm. "Oh Oscar, I do not know where to
turn. He has left me, he says he never wanted a baby, never wanted me fully. He
was just here to pay me to love him and leave him." She began to cry, "I do not
care. You are a filthy whore in my eyes. Scum of the Earth. I do not want you
either, and I do not want some other man's baby, some other man's whore."
"After all we have been through? After all my mother and I did for you in the
Circus? After everything?"
"I was left the Circus, did you know that? Colton left it to me! I gave it to
Thomas and Iris, maybe if you go back to them, they will have some sympathy. I
do not, I will not. Get out of my office." She stood, tears rolling down her cheeks,
"and, Catherine, if I ever see you again, I will kill you." A look of fear and pain
crossed her face, she knew I was serious in my threat. "Fine then. Goodbye
Oscar." She turned and left the office. As she left, I noticed an envelope on the
floor just inside the door. I picked it up, opened up. My stomach dropped.

"I know what you have done."

Chapter Fourteen

I did not know what to think about said letter I had found. If anyone knew what I had done, they would have turned me in by now with the reward being as high as it is for the lucky one to find Jack the Ripper. I went back down the hall, "Nurse, besides my estranged wife, which if she ever shows up here again, turn her away, was there anyone else who came through?" The nurse shook her head, "Not that I have seen today, Doctor Melvin. May I ask why?"
"Something was left in my office and I am just trying to figure out who may have left it." She looked concerned, "Anything to be alarmed about?"
"No, nothing to be alarmed about, I just did not know who may have left the note for me, thank you Nurse." My ears were ringing. There was absolutely no way that someone had seen me, why had they not come forward sooner? The police would be all over this and the reward was so high, no one in their right mind would turn down catching Jack the Ripper. No one could place me at the scene of the crimes. No one had been following me around, no one had gone to the police. I finished my work with the old familiar feeling that I was being watched, even in my office that had no windows. I checked on my patients and headed home for the night, too paranoid to even scope out any potential targets, determined to find out who had left the letter in my office.

I returned home to another note left on my door.

"Those women were my friends."

So, this was a prostitute who claims to have seen me? A piece of worthless swine just like those I had killed, or is it Catherine? Is that the real reason she had returned? She was the only one the nurse had let in that day, the only one to have been seen leaving my office. Had she dropped the note? Is she trying to blackmail me now that she was hard up? She was dumber than I thought. I spent the evening at home, curtains drawn. No one was going to be able to place me anywhere. I decided to catch up on that day's post. I could not have been more surprised to see that Martin and Anna Melvin would be putting on a final show here in Whitechapel at the local theatre. I could not believe they were still performing, much less, still alive. I knew at once that I had to attend this show.

A few days later, I walked into the local theatre for the matinee, I had not been this nervous in a long time and I had murdered people. I had not been in a theatre in quite a few years and I had not seen my parents since I was a child. Being completely honest, I had the hopes that I would see Elizabeth at the performance. I was curious as to see if she and my brothers had taken over or become part of the act, I took my seat in the center row as the lights dimmed, they still pulled a large crowd. Maybe they would see me, maybe the would recognize me, maybe they would not.

My mother took center stage, the piano started and she began to sing. A lovely, morose tune. So much passion, so much emotion. She was greying, but her face still looked young as ever. My father came out, taking her hand. "We would like to thank each and every one of you. We know that most of you here have been with us since the beginning, even the dark years when our son was taken from us. To those of you seeing us for the first time, we welcome you and thank you for joining us on our finale." My father smiled with a bow. I could not believe they had used me all those years ago and still to this day to pull sympathy from the crowd. What a rotten thing to do. It took all of my might not to stand up to expose myself and them for the frauds they were. I decided against it, I would let them have their moment. Their performance consisted of acts throughout their years of entertaining, new acts and old ones I remember sneaking down to watch until all hours of the night. It was a bittersweet time.

As my parents took their finale bows to a roaring standing ovation, I decided it was time to have my moment. I discretely made my way back to the dressing area and waited until they had disappeared into their dressing room.

I could hear voices as I worked up the courage to knock on the door. My father's getting closer, "Oh, Anna, it was a-" his voice cut off as he opened the door, a look of surprised confusion on his face. "Martin, who is at the door?" I made my way inside without an invitation, pushing passed my father, Anna, my mother was sitting at her vanity taking her show jewelry off, her eyes widened and she turned around once she saw me in the mirror, "Oscar, my boy. Is that you?" She stood up, taking a few steps towards me, I backed up. "Yes it is I, do not call me your boy." Her eyes welled with tears, "I can not believe you are here, it has been so long. You have finally come home to us?" She smiled, "Do not toy with me, Anna. I know what you did when we went to the Circus, I know that you were paid for Colton to kidnap me." My mother looked to my father, he just looked to the floor. "I see, Son."

"Do not call me that, you gave that right away, you sold that right when you sold me."

"Oscar, you do not understand. We did it for your own good." I scoffed, "You did it for YOUR own good, you never gave a damn about me. You hated me from the moment I was born, your own words. You called me a monster just because of the way I looked, you let Peter and James tease and taunt me, forbid my siblings to speak to me, made me your slave, starved me to the point where Elizabeth would sneak down late at night and share her own dinner with me." They exchanged glances once again, "You gave me away, no sold me to a horrible, disgusting piece of human filth. He beat me when I was a child, he stuck me in a cage with a live tiger and then used me as a freak in his side show. He whipped me until I passed out, he made money off of me for people to gawk. All because the two of you were scared you would lose your precious social standing. Because the two of you were, and from tonight's showing as you used my disappearance to pull pity and sympathy from your fans, you still are just as bad as Colton. When he died, he left me the Circus, I despised the place so much I gave it to someone, I did not care about the money it could bring in for me. You ruined me as a person. I have now become the monster you so deemed me."

My mother had began to cry, "Oscar, it is not that simple. Yes, we sold you to keep people from finding out you belonged to us. We would have lost everything if anyone had found out."

"That is the worst lie you could ever tell. I made a man millions of dollars because of how I looked, I inherited a fortune and gave it all away because I despised that man so much. I am now a successful surgeon who is helping the police examine crime scenes, I am successful despite the way I look."

"Oscar, we can not tell you how sorry we are for what we did. We have thought about you every day. We did truly love you." I laughed, a good hearty laugh. "You did not love me. I came here to show you that I became a better person than I ever would have been had you not gotten rid of me. Tell Elizabeth I say hello and thank her for being the only person to care for me, to actually love me." My mother looked as if I had smacked her in the face, "Son, er, Oscar, we do not know where Elizabeth is. She ran away not too long after Colton took you. We have not heard from her in quite a few years. Your brothers left us not too long after as well." It was almost too fitting that these people who were my parents, who treated my siblings like they were gold and I like a piece of trash were now standing with me, the only child to make a visit as an adult. "I am not here to make peace with you, I am not here to reconcile. I am not here to forgive you, I only came to show you that I am fine. You can move on and enjoy your life." I pushed passed my father, making my way from the dressing room, slamming the door behind me. It was not the way I wanted the meeting to go, I wanted to scream and scare them and make them feel horrible in the same way they made me feel when I found out they had sold me. I hope I had gotten my message across to them.

I was so riled up after leaving, I decided to take a walk. I made my way towards the tea shop that the lovely Molly who was now a corpse in pieces owned, to my shock, it was open. I poked my way inside, "Good Day Sir," a young girl behind the counter with fiery red hair and piercing green eyes smiled at me, "Hello Miss." "What can I do you for?" I looked around, "Is this the tea shop that Molly owned?" Her smile slightly faded, "Yes, Sir. Did you know Molly?" I was not sure what to say to this young girl who was most likely related to Molly in some way, "I had recently met her and became sort of a regular here. I liked to come and unwind after a hard day at work. Molly was always so kind and always offered up wonderful conversation." The girl nodded, "Yes, my sister was a special girl. Did not know a stranger nor an enemy. She was loved by all." Her words hit me straight in the stomach. For the first time, I actually felt guilty for what I had done to one of my victims. Molly had done nothing to anyone, nothing to hurt anyone or make anyone feel bad about themselves. She just got caught in my own selfish outlook, my own selfish agenda to hurt those who had hurt others. "Well, I do not know if I can offer as wonderful conversation as Molly, but you are welcome to sit and have some tea if you would like."

"Thank you, Miss. I think I shall."

"My name is Mary." I nodded with a smile, "Oscar."

"Pleased, go ahead and grab a seat, I will get some tea going." She disappeared into the back room, I took a seat at my normal table, I had only used once or twice before killing Molly. For one of the few times in my life, I said a little prayer. A prayer for the dear Molly and myself. I knew I would continue to murder, possibly until the point I would get caught. If I ever did get caught. Who was to say I would? "So, Oscar, what do you do for a living around here?" Mary popped back over with the tea kettle, "I am a surgeon at the local medical center."

"Oh, fancy man saving lives then, eh?" I shrugged, "I guess so." I still preferred to take lives rather than save them. I like your hat you got there, she smiled. "My sister made it for me when I was a bit younger. Helps me think." I winked at her, with a slight smile. "So, did you take over the business after Molly, well, umm, I am not sure how to finish this sentence without sounding disrespectful."

"After Molly passed? I was not going to, but I thought it may be a nice way to keep her memory and to honor her." She looked around, "I have come in and helped before, learned the business pretty good. I mean, it is just making tea and biscuits. What is to be so hard about that?" She giggled, a most wonderful sound. "Well, you never know. I do not think I could make a decent cup of tea, alas why I started coming in here. Then, I kept coming in for Molly. She as a dear woman. I am sorry that she was taken from you." Mary nodded, "Thank you, that is kind." We sat in silence for a few moments, both looking out the window into the streets, busy for the time being. Finally, Mary spoke up, breaking into my thoughts.

"What do you like to do in your free time?" I shrugged, "Well, I do not take much free time anymore. After my wife and I separated, I put myself into my work most of the time."

"I am sorry to hear of your separation. Times seem to be hard these days, gets the best of the best people." I nodded, "and lately I have been helping the Inspectors on these murders which takes up a lot of time as well." She looked up at me, I tried to avoid her eyes, "Oh, you were at Molly's examination then?"

"I was." I looked at Mary, "We do not have to speak of Molly. I can see that it is still a hard time for you." She nodded, "Yes, it was very hard to hear that she was murdered, especially in such a way. I had to identify the body with Inspector Abberline. He was not as comforting as you have been." I laughed slightly, "He is not a very comforting man, very hard, but also very determined to catch this man." Mary smiled, "Well, I guess that is a good thing then. I hope they catch him and hang him in the square for all to see." I almost choked on my tea. I felt it was my time to make my leave. I stood, "Well, Mary, it was lovely to meet you. I should get back to the center and get back to saving lives. I shall stop in again, if I have not over stayed my welcome."

"Nonsense. It would be nice to have you stop by any time. Your words have been very kind, I do hope you can help solve these murders. The world is so upside down right now." I took her hand, "It will get better, I promise. Have faith." She smiled as I made my way through the door.

I caught the evening post as I walked in the door to the medical center, I thought it a good time to send another letter in, this one for those fools who say they have seen me, those fools who say they can give a description and then give a description of almost every male there is today. I grabbed a quill and some ink, sprawling the words out.

"You thought your-self very clever I reckon when you informed the police. But you made a mistake if you though I dident see you. Now I known you know me and I see your little game, and I mean to finish you and send your ears to your wife if you show this to the police or help them if you do I will finish you. It no use your trying to get out of my way. Because I have you when you dont expect it and I keep my word as you soon see and rip you up. Yours truly Jack the Ripper.

PS You see I know your address"

I leaned back in my chair, I knew the local paper would print the letter, they loved to help me to keep my name out there, keep them on their toes and remind the public they had not caught Jack the Ripper and they most likely never would. It was almost exhausting to do the police work for them to lead them off of my trail. I needed to take out more of these hookers. I would make it my life's work to rid the world of as many of them as I could using my respectable surgeon face as a cover. As I had no patients, I decided to take the letter immediately instead of later, that way I could be back before what was being called Ripper Time. I made a few stops for supplies for the upcoming weeks, dropped the letter, took a short walk for some fresh air before returning to the center, I checked in with the nurse to put myself on call if needed, made my way to my quarters, turning in for the night.

I awoke early the next morning to check out the paper, there were two articles that caught my attention. The first was of course, my letter. They had it printed on the front page, which I would definitely be adding to my collection of front page headlines. The other was an article from a Mister Lusk, the so called President of the Whitechapel Vigilance Committee. He decided to make a statement to Good Old Jack.

"We will find this man, this vigilante who is out there murdering these women. We have the man power to help the police, we will put men on every corner at every time of the day and through the night. He will not escape us much longer, even if he does find himself to be of such high intelligence. We will have him. We will give these women the justice they so deserve, as well as closure to their families."

Justice to whores? Closure to their families? You mean the families who deserted them, the husbands they cheated on, the children they abandoned, the parents they fought with and left? You want closure for all of these rotten people? Oh, Mister

Lusk, I have a surprise for you. I will show you just how intelligent I am and that you will never catch me. I would send Lusk a package of my own. A very special package from me to him. I went into my quarters where I was still hiding the body parts from one Catherine Eddowes, pulled the jars out from the fake panel I installed in the wall behind my bookshelf and cut part of the kidney away, wrapping it in a piece of thick sheet so it would not leak, put it in a box and penned a little note.

From Hell.
Mr Lusk,
Sor
I send you half the kidne I took from one woman and prasarved it for you tother piece I fried and ate it was very nise. I may send you the bloody knif that took it out if you only wate a whil longer

signed
catch me when you can Mishter Lusk

I would get the better of this man, this man who thought he could outwit me, out talk me. I had all the odds in my favor at this moment. Abberline was starting to trust me, he had me stepping in to investigations and the murder scenes, even the mortuary examinations. I was right under their noses and they still could not catch me. Fools. I put the box in my bag and made my way once again down to the post. Dropped it into the free standing box, I could not chance anyone seeing me with this box as I knew it would become high profile news. I was very proud of myself. My good mood ended when I returned to my office to find another note left for me by whomever it was claiming to know I was the Ripper. I opened it not amused in the slightest.

You will pay for what you have done.
Either in pounds or in public shame.

So, now they were interested in blackmail. This would not fly with me. I had no way to get in touch with this person to even inquire about their demands. I guess I would just have to wait for their next attempt at contact.

Chapter Fifteen

I could not stop thinking about Mary and how sad she was. I felt guilty for taking her sister from her, her lovely well put together sister, a woman who just happened to be at the wrong place and the wrong time. For her anyway, for me it was wonderfully placed timing. I wanted to ask Mary out for a dinner to cheer up a little bit.

I grabbed my coat and went to the little tea shop, "Good Morning, Doctor Melvin."
"Mary, please, call me Oscar." She smiled, "I am sorry, I am just trying to be respectful to your title."
"I do respect that, but please, you met me as Oscar, I will not accept anything more than that title." She nodded, "What can I get for you today?" I felt a bit nervous, I had only ever been out with Catherine and that had been a long time ago. To have someone I was even thinking about asking out, even as friends was making my heart pound. "Mary, I would like to take you out for dinner," her eyes widened, "As friends, of course, just to cheer you up a bit. I know what it is like to lose a sibling you love and care deeply about." Mary smiled while in thought, "I guess that would be fine." I smiled, "Great, how does tomorrow evening sound? There is a little cafe not too far from here I have been wanting to try out." She nodded, "Sounds great. Can I get you some tea?" I shook my head, "Not today, I have a lot of work to get done, I just wanted to stop in and say hello." She waved, "Well, hello."
"And, farewell for today." Her spirits seemed to be lifted as left the shop, I was not sure what I hoped would happen the next evening. Did I want this to become something more than two friends going out for a dinner? I was not quite ready for anything with anyone new. I needed to put my mind elsewhere and just go with the times.

I noticed the letter before I even made it halfway up the walk to my house. Was this from my little friend?

I will be in touch soon as to where you can find me.

Was this person serious? Who tries to blackmail a murderer? Someone who had already killed four women and was not about to stop. I laughed to myself and went inside, I did not have time for these nonsense games. I was on a mission. I needed to get my best together for tomorrow. I would not be going out this evening, I had plenty of time to find other whores, they seemed to just walk into my arms most nights.

I showed up to the Tea shop around five o'clock. Mary had decided to close early so we could have a nice dinner. On my way, I stopped by to pick up some flowers for her. A lovely assortment of what the flower shop owner called carnations and lilies, I remembered her mentioning they were her favorite. She smiled when she saw me as she was locking the shop doors. "Well, just a friendly dinner, eh?" I shrugged, "I still want to make it a special one." She smiled, "Well, thank you. They are lovely. My favorites."
"I remember you saying that you wanted to have a garden full of nothing but carnations and lilies." She perked her head to the side, "I do. I think it would make for a beautiful sight." She took my arm as we walked towards the small cafe.

"So, tell me more about yourself. All I know about you is that you are a surgeon helping the police. What was your childhood like?" Mary asked as we took our seats, I hesitated, "Well, my childhood was not a good one. I had parents who thought of me as a monster from the moment I was born." Mary's face fell, "Why on Earth would anyone think a newborn was a monster?" I took my hat off, I was going to have everything out in the open with Mary. She looked at the large deformity on my head, "Oh, my." was all she could muster to say, "I was born with it. They treated me a lot like a slave, less like a son. I cooked, cleaned, did all the house chores with the servants. They did not want anyone to know I was their son so they hid me away. I was teased and taunted a lot by my siblings. At ten years old, I was sold to the Circus where I grew up a sideshow performer. I studied my life away as a child to make something of myself so I could leave that life as soon as I was able." Mary looked instantly uncomfortable, "Oscar, I, um, I have no idea what to say. Is that how you lost your siblings?" I nodded, looking at the table, "My sister Elizabeth was the only person who made me feel loved, accepted, human. She was the last person I saw before I was taken. The look of fear and horror on her face haunts me to this day." I looked up at Mary who had an expression that showed she was feeling very awkward. "I am sorry, I really should not have dropped all of this on you." She shook her head as if trying to wake herself up from a trance. "No, do not be sorry, I asked. I mean, I told you to tell me about yourself, you did. I just had no idea that your family was so horrible to you."
"My parents were show folk, I actually came from their last and final show when I came in to the tea shop the other day. I saw in the paper they were ending their career, I took to their matinee. I ended up going to their dressing room after and confronting them." I was not sure why I was telling Mary all of this, I felt that if I had not ruined the friendship already, this would do it. "I bet that was interesting." I laughed, "For lack of a better word, yes. They told me that my sister had run away not too long after I had disappeared and they had not heard from her for years, so they could not even tell me if she was still alive." Mary looked down, "I

87

do hope she is." There was a long silence as we waited for the waiter to take our order, "I am sorry if I ruined this dinner." Mary laughed, "It is not ruined." "Why don't you tell me about yourself, lighten it up a little bit." Mary wiped her mouth, "Well, I grew up in a pretty wealthy family. Nothing special, I had three siblings, Molly was who I was closest to. I spent a lot of time studying and traveling, my mother liked to go anywhere and everywhere she could and would take us with her. That is pretty much it. I have not really done much in life." I laughed, "Well, simple gal. Nothing wrong with that." Mary nodded, "Yes, simple." We talked about many different things through dinner, things we wanted to do in the future, places we wanted to visit, people we thought would be fun to meet. It took me back to my nights with Elizabeth, when she would sneak down and talk to me. It was a great end to a perfectly awkward start. We took the long way around to her home so we could chat a little more and see some of the sights, even though it was a mighty cold October night. "Well, this is mine here," she stopped at a small cottage, "Do get home safe. Thank you for dinner, thank you for the flowers, they are stunning." She kissed my cheek, turned and walked up her drive. I watched to make sure she got in safely and then continued on my way back home.

I had the feeling I was being followed, I had always felt this way ever since the Circus. I listened hard to try to hear if there were any footsteps behind me, I confirmed there were. I acted none the wiser, enjoying the chilly night air. When I got a little closer to my home, I turned sharply. Seeing the figure of a woman not too far behind me, "You know, it is not very wise to sneak around behind people when there is a killer on the loose."

"How do you know I am not the killer?" I laughed, "That really is not the point, I could have easily taken you out myself many times on our game of cat and mouse." She scoffed, "I know who you are. I know what you have done."

"Who do you think I am?"

"You know that you are the Ripper. You know you have been killing off my friends, the only people I have in this world," her voice was timid, she sounded younger when she tried to act tough. "If you feel I am the Ripper, how is it you have not gone to the police about me? How is it that you are stalking me at this hour? I do not believe I would approach someone I thought to be a killer in the middle of the night."

"You are more vital to me not in prison, not hanged for all to see. That is what they will do you when they catch you."

"They will not catch me. I control the knowledge of the murders that they receive." Another scoff, "I will go to them, I will tell them all about everything that I have seen." She stepped a little closer, she was tall for a woman, around my height, stout. Her hair was golden from what I could tell when she stepped into the light, she was not intimidating in any way, shape, or form. I knew the odds were in my favor. "Unless you want to help me."

"Help you how?" I was curious as to what she was going to ask for, I knew all too well money would be on the list if it was not the only thing she was after. "Well, living this life is hard. I make my ends meet, but if I had someone paying me to keep quiet, I would be quite a bit more comfortable." I laughed, "You want me to pay you to keep quiet on something you can not prove?" The anger in her voice began to show.

"Oh, they will not care about proof when I squeal. They are just looking for someone to put away, to blame, to kill for these murders." She stepped closer, I went on the defense. I had only a small clasp knife in my pocket, "I will not let you blackmail me. Also, if you keep bothering me, I will kill you myself." I made sure to sound firm and final. I turned and continued on my way home. The whore was not going to get me to show any kind of anger or rage towards her, no matter how much it was ready to burst out of me right now. I would get her, I did not know when, but I would get her. How dare she think she can get me caught? My blood was on fire when I finally reached my home. I immediately began to pour myself glass after glass of gin.

I awoke a few hours later after passing out from my angry drunken stupor to someone banging on my door, I had a feeling I knew who it would be before even opening the door. "Doctor Melvin? You look horrible." Abberline stood on the stoop outside, "Just putting in long days at the center, how can I help you, Detective?"

"Well, we have had someone come in to the station and claim they know who the Ripper is." I tried to look as surprised as I could in my state, "Oh, have you now? That is an interesting claim. Who are they pointing at?" Abberline cleared his throat, looking a little uncomfortable, "I hate to say but they are pointing at you, Doctor." I blinked my eyes a few times to look alarmed, "Me? Why on Earth would anyone point the finger at me?"

"I am not sure but we do need to take all accusations on this matter quite seriously. I need you to come down to the station with me," I tried to look as outraged as possible but that I would cooperate as much as I could, "I understand, Detective. Let me get my coat and hat." He nodded, I took a few deep breaths, this trip into the station could make or break me. I had to get this act down just right, I could not let them see any of myself falter. I walked out to the wagon and hopped in, Abberline sat next to me, "I am very sorry that we have to do this to you, Son. We just can not be too careful." I nodded, "I am just trying to figure out why someone would accuse you of all people. A bright, young surgeon on his way up in the world."

"Maybe that is why they are doing it, was it that Doctor Brown? He does not seem to like me very much." Abberline stifled a laugh, "No, he does not, but it also was not him." I shrugged, "It does not really matter who it is, I will clear my name. I have an alibi for two of the murders and the others, you can ask my neighbors, I was at home the nights of the others, you even came to get me." He nodded, "Just a few simple questions, a simple line up for the witness to say yes or no and you will be back on your way home." I laughed, "Is it that simple? What if this witness says it is me that they saw and yet, I have about five people who say otherwise?"

"We will deal with it, this is all procedure." I nodded.

We pulled up to the police station, a crowd had began to form. "Word travels quickly, Detective." He shook his head, "No one should know anything about this." We both emerged from the wagon, "MURDERER!" someone yelled from the crowd, "People, we have not confirmed this man to be the killer, he has a clad tight alibi for the murders, he has also been helping with the investigation. We feel this is someone who is just trying to ruin his reputation and career. Please, return home and details will be released tomorrow." The crowd booed and did not move from their spot. Abberline pushed a way through the crowd, "Whoever tipped off the press and the people who are now waiting outside will be in big trouble when I find out!" he yelled when we entered the station. He took me into a room with an officer and a few other men with looks and builds similar to my own. I could not believe I could possibly be caught tonight, that this was about to happen. This whore would call on me, of course she would, she already told me that she was going to the police about me. I would have to jump through hoops to clear my name and I would but Abberline would most likely be on my case from here on out. I needed a plan and quick.

Chapter Sixteen

They left us to sit in the small room for what seemed like a few hours, then an officer came in and had us all stand against the wall. We had to turn to the left, turn to the right, and turn to the back. All of us wearing a long coat and top hat, of course, the other men were sent away as I was asked to stay. Detective Abberline came in a few moments later, "I am sure by now you realize that the witness has pointed you out as the person they saw at the scenes. "Detective, if I may ask, how does this person claim to have seen me at every murder? Was this person at every murder? I find this to be suspicious," I tried to sound like an innocent man, "I understand your plight, we are taking this matter seriously. I know that you have alibis, we have already spoken to the night nurse and your neighbors. I made sure to have all bases covered before we went through with the line up test. We will be releasing you but we must first go through the motions so it does not seem as if we were favoring you." I nodded, still unsure if I would be sent home or if I would end up in a cell. Abberline left the room. I sat there, nervously awaiting someone to come get me. I felt as if my chest was about to burst open to spill all of the contents everywhere. Just when I felt I had been done in, Abberline opened the door, "You are free to go, Son. Do you want a ride back to the center or home?" I stood, shaking my head, "No, thank you. I will walk."
"Are you sure that is safe? There are a lot of people who will think you are guilty. I do not want your safety to be jeopardized." I waved him off, "I promise, I will be fine." He looked worried but let me go anyway. I made my way out of the station, taking in the deepest breath of my life once I reached outside. I could have thrown up the entire dinner I had eaten earlier. I made my way home, "Dirty whore." A voice came from my left, "I beg your pardon?"
"That is what they called me. A dirty whore. A dirty whore with no real solid proof, a dirty whore just trying to get you in trouble. These men are just as twisted as you. Protecting a murderer, pigs." I laughed, "Did I not tell you that I would not be apprehended? Did I not tell you that you had nothing against me. All you did was bring attention to yourself as someone who was at every murder scene while I have people who can back where I was to the police." She sniffled, I could tell she was crying. She was no match for someone like me, someone who had no sympathy or remorse for anything. A monster. She still cared for these women who were gone at the strike of my hand. She had to be dealt with, she would definitely be my next target. I would learn her ways, without her ever knowing, I would have her gone before the end of the year. "I can not believe you will get away with this, with what you have done." She spit at me then she turned and disappeared into the night.

I returned to the medical center, I felt it was safer than returning home until this all died down, "Doctor Melvin, I heard what happened. Are you all right?" I nodded,

"Yes, thank you Victoria. Just someone trying to ruin my reputation. I have cleared my name with the police." She smiled slightly, "Oh, that is good news. I am very happy to hear that." I nodded, "Thank you, I will be in my quarters, I have had a long evening. If you need me, please get me." She nodded, "Get some rest, Doctor." Once in my room, I saw the post with the investigation on the kidney piece I had sent to Mister Lusk. He had Doctor Openshaw take a look at it, simple statement. The piece was from the left kidney of who they assumed to be Catherine Eddowes, the most gruesome murder as of yet. I would show them, my next victim was already hand picked, she pretty much presented herself to me as someone who wanted to be killed. I would make an example of her, no one would accuse me of murder and get away with it. She could have ruined everything for me, my career, my life. She would not get away with it. And, as I had already cleared my name, they would never link it back to me. I almost perfected my craft.

I sat down and wrote a letter before going to sleep, I would send it to Doctor Openshaw to congratulate him for being able to tell it was the left kidney. He was a superb doctor.

Old boss you was rite it was the left kidny i was goin to hoperate agin close to you ospitle just as i was going to dror mi nife along of er bloomin throte them cusses of coppers spoilt the game but
i guess i wil be on the jobn soon and will send you another bit of innerds

Jack the Ripper

O have you seen the devle with his mikerscope and scalpul a-lookin at a kidney with a slide cocked up.

I was so exhausted from the day I had, I decided to send the letter out the next day. Doctor Openshaw never liked me, just like Doctor Brown. They did not take well to a younger doctor coming in and helping out with the investigations and the scenes as they wanted the glory for themselves. Old coots. I hoped that I would never get as old as them and if I did, I would not be like that. I am always welcoming new and upcoming methods and new and upcoming surgeons. I want people to take over after I am gone, I want the medical field to flourish, to advance. I wanted lives to continue to be saved as I continued to take them. I felt I would bring my time to an end soon though, only because I did not want to push my luck. I could go on forever murdering filthy women but I had so many close calls that I was not keen to keep barely getting by. If so much kept coming back to me, sooner or later Abberline would get wise and he would finally arrest me. Even though he had no proof and nothing to make anything stick, I did not want the trouble. I began to feel sticky and trapped, I told Victoria I needed to get out. I made my way out into the world, I thought maybe a walk would be good for me, I walked by the tea shop, Mary was sitting in the window which I thought was odd

considering I dropped her off at home a few hours before. I knocked and waved, she gave me an unpleasant look but waved back. I pointed towards the door, she came out to me. "Why are you out here so late? You know you should be careful." She wrapped her shawl around her, "I know. I just, I wanted to retrace Molly's steps, or what I imagine what would have been the steps she took before she died." I was taken aback. "Why in the world would you want to do that? Why would you torture yourself so?" She began to cry, "I need to find her killer and if I can figure out where she went after she closed up, I can possibly find a clue. Anything to lead me to her murderer." I still wonder if I should have reached out and pulled her into my arms or not, I did not at the time. I was not sure how she would react and I did not want to push her into anything she was uncomfortable with. "Mary, I know she was your sister and you love her but you can not do this. You can not do this to yourself, and how do you think she would feel if she knew you were putting yourself in danger in such a way to find someone who may not even still be in the area?" She looked at me, another unpleasant look. "I can not give up on her, you do not understand, you did not have your siblings growing up to get close to, to love, to do anything for! Just go home Oscar!" It was as if she had punched me in the gut with her words, she went back inside the shop, slamming the door behind her and turning off the lights. I stood in a stupor for a moment, I had not fully processed what had happened. I was only trying to look out for her safety and also to keep her from finding something that could lead the murder to me, which I knew would never be found, but I did not want to take the chance that I was the only person out here hurting women. Just because women were not being killed does not mean other horrible acts were not being committed against them. "Your pretty little friend mad at you?" I turned to once again encounter the woman who had been following me, my accuser. "You are not a very smart woman are you?" She laughed, a ferocious vile laugh. "I am a very smart woman, I knew who you were did I not?" "Yes, and you turned the police against you by doing something stupid." "What are her knickers all wound up about?"
"None of your business." I began to walk back to the medical center, the woman right on my trail. "You know, you have not even asked me name. I would think you would want to know who I am so when the time is right you can find me." I kept walking, ignoring her foolish words. I needed to keep to myself in case we ended up passing people out and about, it would look as if she was harassing me. I said nothing else to her for the rest of the trip to the medical center, I closed the door on her laughing at me. "There are some weird folks in this world." I said to myself, "There most certainly are, Doctor." Victoria was sitting at the nurses' station, smiling at me. "This woman just followed me for like six blocks harassing me. She is the one who accused me as a murderer. Does that make sense to you? If I was a murderer, I could have taken her out easily." Victoria laughed, "Oh, Doctor Melvin, someone as kind as you could never be a murderer. You save lives, you do not take them." I held my laugh in, this woman had no clue. I nodded at her and proceeded to my quarters. I needed sleep.

The next morning was a tough one, I was not prepared for the events that would come before me. I was woken up by Nurse Trighter knocking on my door. "Doctor, sorry to bother you, I know you are not on yet but we have an emergency."
"What happened?" I followed her down the hallway, passed the recovery rooms into the operating room. "She was brought in by a woman who did not want to identify herself, she said she would want you to be the one to help her." I looked at the woman on the table.

Mary.

My heart sank, her wrists had been cut with a razor. "Is she breathing?" I raced to the table, "Mary. Mary, can you hear me?" I said loudly, Mary stirred a little but was not responding. I went to work right away, trying to stop the bleeding so I could stitch the open wounds. "Nurse, what did the woman who brought her in look like?" The nurse stared at me wide eyed, "She had...she had..."
"Was she blonde? Tall? A little broad?" The nurse nodded, "Yes, Doctor. Do you think she did this to her?" I nodded, "I do, and we need to get Detective Abberline here immediately!" The nurse ran from the room to send someone to fetch Detective Abberline. "Hold on for me Mary, I am going to help you. You are going to be okay." Her eyes closed, she was unconscious. I had my secondary nurse help me with the bleeding on one wrist as I stitched up the other. I could not believe this was happening, it angered me and brought the rage back. I had to keep my wits about me. This was the hardest surgery I had ever had to perform. This was not supposed to happen, Mary was not supposed to be on my table. She was supposed to be mad at me and never want to see me again. She should have been on her way to somewhere beautiful, somewhere she could forget all about this dark and dreary place. Somewhere she could forget about me. I had come to terms that I may never see her again and this was definitely not the way I wanted to see her.

It took almost an hour to get both of her wrists stitched up, the cuts were deep. She would be critical but I was hopeful, I had faith she would make a full recovery. I sat with her for a few hours in the recovery wing before I had to get up and move around. She would be resting for a while and I could not stand to see her the way she was, just lying there probably in pain. Maybe she was in a beautiful place in her sleep, not aware of what had happened to her. I grabbed my coat and a few supplies, heading out into the cold. It was a crisp November night, I needed to start trailing my new victim, my filthy whore who had just put a target on her back for good. I could overlook her following me, I could overlook her harassing me, I could even overlook her turning me in to the police and putting me through the trouble of having to clear my name. I would absolutely not overlook her assaulting and almost killing an innocent bystander of the whole thing. Someone who had already been hurting enough, someone who had nothing to do with any of this. I was determined to find her, I was determined to kill her. I was determined to ruin her.

It did not take me long to find her, whatever the worthless piece of filth's name was. She did not deserve the courtesy of me even caring enough to find out. I had seen her, she had not seen me. I trailed her for a few blocks, watching her every move, her every stop. I took mental note of who she spoke to, what she ate, what she drink, and how she moved. I could tell she was a paranoid person, she was very fidgety and kept looking around. Maybe she felt she was being watched as she was. I thought it best not to make my move tonight and returned to the center with a good amount of knowledge of my new prey. Mary was awake when I went in to check on her, she seemed to be a completely different person. I extended a smile to her as I approached her bedside. "Oh, Oscar. I am so terribly embarrassed and sorry. You were right, I should not have been out there that late." I put my hands up, "Hey, hey, hey. No, this is not how we will start this conversation. This is not about being right or wrong. This is about how you are feeling, that you are alive and that you will make a full recovery." She looked down, "I was attacked, I do not know by whom. I was grabbed from behind and I had something cover my face, I could not breathe and then everything went hazy. I was awake but I could not control anything, I could not move and they..." "Shh, Mary. I know what happened, well not fully but I know the details from your injuries. We do not need to speak of it." She looked at her bandaged wrists, "Did you do this?" I shrank, "If by stitch your wounds, yes, but I did not attack you." Her eyes widened as she looked ashamed, "I would never think that you would attack me, Oscar. You have been nothing but respectful, I should have worded that better, I am very sorry I gave you that impression." I shook my head, "You are just fine. I am just happy that you were brought here in time for me to save you, those cuts were deep. I am grateful the person had you somewhat sedated, that would have lowered the feeling of pain if you felt any at all." She shrugged, "Not much really. It was more pressure but I could feel my body getting weaker and weaker once it was done." Mary wiped a tear, "You are safe now. Were you able to speak with Detective Abberline?" A nod. "I could not tell him much but he said he would look into it, that he would take someone to investigate the tea shop and the area around it. I can not believe I did something so stupid." I shook my head, "Do not think any more of it tonight. I want you to get some rest. Do you need anything for the pain?"
"No, I am okay. More tired than anything." I nodded, "You will probably feel groggy for a few days but as I said, I am sure you will make a full recovery."
"Oscar, I must thank you for saving my life and I must apologize. I was so mean to you before, I was just upset and did not know what to say to you and I am sorry."
"I told you, we are not to talk about that. You get some rest, we will see how you feel in the morning." I smiled, she took my hand and gave a light squeeze.

I left the recovery wing and was greeted by Detective Abberline waiting for me, "Doctor."

"Detective." I motioned for him to follow me to my office, "I wanted to speak to you when I came by earlier to get the girl's statement." I nodded, "I needed to get out, I needed to clear my head. I know her and it was a shock to me to see someone I care for like that." Abberline nodded, "I can only imagine, my boy. The nurse told me you were rather distraught, I thought I would come back and check on you. Especially due to the circumstances, I believe the person who did this to Mary is the same person who has been harassing you. The same woman who tried to accuse you of the murders." I tried to act surprised as he had never told me the gender of the person accusing me, "So, it is a woman who came to you?" He nodded, "Yes, a woman who claims to have been friends with the women killed. That is why she is so ruthless in finding the murderer." I nodded, furrowing my brow, "Detective, I am not one to throw around false accusations, but do we think maybe this woman murdered them? I would not put it passed anyone to do these things, if she was at every crime scene, she also could be the one to have sent all of these letters to people involved." He looked like he was simply at a loss, "I just can not be sure, we have nothing to go on. Not the smallest piece of evidence. I promised the city I would find this person and even the evidence pointing towards her, it is all guessing." I nodded, "Well, we will continue to look." He sighed, looked down trodden as he took his leave.

A few days later, Mary was ready to go home. I knew I had to take care of the woman who did this to her before she got a hold of her and did something to hurt her again, or maybe even kill her. "Mary, if this is not too forthcoming, would you feel safer to stay in my home? I have plenty of room and I think it would do my conscience some good to know you were safe." Mary smiled, "Oh, Oscar. Do you think I will ever be fully safe while this crazy lunatic is out on the street? I am grateful for you, I am grateful for the offer but I can not put you out any more than I already have."
"You would not be putting me out, you would be honoring me the chance to make up for not hanging around just a little longer to make sure you made it home okay that night." She smiled weakly. I could tell she was thinking the offer over, she finally looked at me, "Maybe for a few days, until I can get fully functional with my hands, I am still scared to put too much pressure on them." I smiled, "It is settled then. Tomorrow, we will get you out of here." "Are you sure this is no problem?" I shook my head, "Not in the slightest." She touched my face gently, "You are a very good man, Oscar Melvin. Do not let anyone make you feel any different." I smiled and stood, "Well, I do need to get some paperwork and some errands done. You rest and I will check on you later." She nodded, opening a book. She reminded me much of Eliza at this moment. I headed to my office to finish my paperwork for the day, packed a small supply bag, grabbed my coat and my hat, and made my way out of the office. "Victoria, I need to run a few errands, I am going to have Mary stay with me until she is fully recovered, please keep an eye on her. No one goes in there unless it is Detective Abberline, myself or a center staff. Is that understood?" Victoria nodded with a sly grin on her face, "And, get rid of that smug grin, it is nothing more than a friend taking care of a friend." She laughed, "Sure, Doctor Melvin, whatever you say."

It was a chilly night, one that cut straight to the bone. I was on my final mission to find this whore and take care of her. She would be gone before the night was over. I took the same walk as I had the night before, she would most likely have the same little beat with the same gentlemen callers. About an hour or so later, I came across her. She was sitting with a man outside a pub, laughing and having a grand time. Enjoy it now, swine. Your hours are numbered. I waited until she made her move and then I made mine. I followed her around the block a few times. She seemed to be unsuccessful in picking up any more customers. She headed back to the residential part of the city. I followed her to Miller's Court, where she let herself in to a room at McCarthy's. I stood and waited in the shadow to see if she was coming back out. It looked as if she was in for the night, I slowly made my way to the door, peeking in the window, she was alone. I tapped lightly on the door and hid around a corner, the door opened a crack, "Ye?" She looked around and then closed the door. I would wait a bit and knock again now knowing she would open up without looking. Around half an hour or so, I made my way back over to the door, tapped lightly as not to bring any attention from outsiders, the door opened a bit and I pushed it in. I made sure to grab her first and cover her mouth so she could not scream. I kicked the door closed, still holding her in my arms, one hand over her mouth, one on her throat. Her eyes were wide with terror. "Did you not think I would come after you? Did you not think I would end you? After all of the nonsense you have pulled with my life? I could have looked passed the foolish antics you pulled with me but to then try to murder my friends? That was the final straw." She kicked at me, getting me in the knee, I lost grip on her mouth, "MURDER!" she managed to scream before I got a good hold on her again. I pulled out the chloroform and let her slip into a hazy stupor. She turned to run from me, tripping over the small chair sitting at her table, probably feeling the effects of the sedative I had just given her, I grabbed her by the hair, smashing her face into the bed post. I was going to let her stay awake and alive for most of what I was about to do to her. Just like she did with Mary. I wanted her to struggle, to fight, and to feel the life leaving her body.

I pulled off her dress revealing her filthy, disgusting naked body. Folding it, I set it to the side. I cut at her right shoulder, taking her arm clean off, leaving it just shy of her body. I pushed her legs wide open, spread apart. I could tell she was feeling somewhat of the things I was doing, she would clench up and then relax, going in and out of consciousness, just out of it enough not to scream. I hacked into her abdomen, taking all of the organs out of her body, she did not deserve any of it. She was not a human being, she was an empty, nasty whore. Void of any emotion, void of any human traits. I sliced her wrists, her arms, and shoulders. I slashed her face, the rage that had been building up inside of me for her finally able to be set free, let out into the open. She was going to be my worst yet, forget Catherine Eddowes, this was my moment. This would end my killing spree, but would keep me alive in legend. I cut into her breasts, taking them completely off then I dug the knife into her neck, that wonderful gurgle began, I cut so deep, I felt the blade hit the bone. I took her uterus and her kidneys and shoved them under her head with her breast, I placed the other by her foot, leaving the liver shoved between her feet. I pulled her intestines and her spleen up and left them by her left side. The rest I left on the table next to the bed. Probably one where she ate daily. There was blood everywhere. I wanted her to be hardly recognizable, hardly able to be identified. I slashed through her lung then literally ripped her heart out. It was not as if she had ever used it. I threw it into the fireplace. It was not as quick of a kill as I would have liked, by the time I was done with everything, I could see light popping up through the curtain. I cleaned up all of the evidence that could lead back to me and I made my way out of the door, checking before to see if anyone was around. I locked the door from the inside and pulled it shut as quietly as I could. I made my way back to the medical center.

A few hours later, Abberline showed up at my door. He looked rather smug, "There has been another murder, I need you to come with me. It is even worse than our others." I nodded, "Let me grab my bag."
"It will not be needed, there is nothing left." I followed the Inspector to the wagon where he led us over to the crime scene. I tried to look as appalled and surprised as I could, but all I could do mentally was revel in the greatness that lied before me. "Detective, this is pretty cut and dry, is there something specific you would like me to look for?" Doctor Bond inquired as he gave me a glance over, "I just need a statement for the report. I am not asking for anything more than that on this one. I can not stomach this today." I took a step inside, the mess was extraordinary. If I were a man of weak stomach, I would have already emptied its contents on the floor. There were officers standing around with their handkerchiefs over their mouths and noses as the body had began to have an odor to it. I nodded slightly at each of them as if to say I understand. I made my way to the body, making notes of everything I already knew. Detective Abberline stood behind me, "It is a horrible sight is it not?" I turned, "It is. I have to agree it is." I began to write down everything I could see as far as body parts and placement of everything. I would definitely have to save a copy of the evening edition of the daily post where I would be giving a statement on a murder I committed myself to help the police investigation. "What is the meaning of this? Who are you people?" A man was pushing his way into the room, "Why are- oh my goodness, Mary?" My head turned quickly, "Do you know this woman, Sir?" Abberline stopped the man, his hands on his chest. "That is my Mary. That is my girl."
"What is her full name?"
"Mary Jane Kelly." He could not pull his eyes away from the corpse. "Sir, we need to back up, we can not have anything happen to the crime scene or evidence." He stepped outside with Abberline to give a full statement. Most of it consisting of him being at work the whole night and having people who could back him up. Abberline came back in, gravely looking at me. I returned his glance as if to ask why he was staring at me in such a manner. "Doctor Melvin, may I speak with you outside?" I followed him to a secluded area away from the rest of the investigators. "Do you recognize that woman at all?" I shook my head, "No, I have never seen her before."

"That is the woman who accused you of being the Ripper." I put on a look of fake shock. I took a moment, staring at the ground and then back at Abberline. "This is, er, was the woman who accused me?" Abberline nodded. I stared at the doorway, trying to make it seem as if I was processing his words. "I do not know what to say, or even think right now. I can not...Sir, can I even be here right now? I do not know how this works."

"I think it is best if you were to maybe head back to the medical center." I nodded, shook his hand. "I will stop by when I am done here." I nodded and walked away, smiling to myself.

I sat at the table with Mary, laughing. I knew Detective Abberline would be by soon once he figured out I was not at the medical center. I wanted to get Mary out of that place. I wanted to get her home. A knock on the door, Abberline. I pulled the door open, welcoming him into the home, "Doctor. Miss." He tipped his hat to Mary, "I am glad to see you have made a full recovery." She smiled, "Thank you, Detective."

"I will only take a moment of your time, but I think I come bearing good news. I feel we have seen the last of the Ripper murders. I believe that Mary Jane Kelly was our Ripper and the man who was at the scene earlier, that she was living with, a Joseph Barnett stumbled upon her secret and in a angry rage murdered her himself. I feel things will go back to normal now." Mary sighed, "For the love of goodness, we can only hope." She came up behind me, put her hand on my back. "You are now cleared of any and all suspicion. I will make a clear and final statement later." Abberline said, "You two have a great afternoon." I nodded and smiled, watching Abberline walk down the drive. That would be the last time I ever saw him. Mary smiled as I turned from closing the door, "Well, shall we carry on with the rest of our lives?" I laughed, "Yes. Yes, I think we shall."

Epilogue

Mary never left me. We enjoyed each other's company and she stayed. We lived happily together up until her death of natural causes four years ago. I miss her dearly, she was the best thing that ever happened to me. She was a blessing as she understood and put up with the fact that we could never get married because I was still legally married to Catherine, whom I never heard from again.

I heard through one of the officers that Detective Inspector Frederick Abberline moved up in the ranks, making it to head of his own station. I heard earlier this year that he himself had passed away. Never finding out who the real Ripper was.

I sit here in my own hell, happy that I have finally put these words to paper, finally removed them from just my memory. Maybe some day someone will read them and they will know the real story.

Thinking back to everything that happened, the circus, the murders, the medical center. I am still proud of myself for never getting caught, had some close calls but I was able to work my way out of them. I am the most famous, no infamous killer of all time. People are still talking about me, I hear them out in the world, I hear the theories. They still fear me. They do not know if I will ever strike again.

I am too old of a man to carry out any of that nonsense now. I will die soon and I welcome that. I will be happy to finally be with my sweet Mary and my sweet Elizabeth again.

Made in the USA
Columbia, SC
20 August 2023